ANN DENTON

LE RUE PUBLISHING

Le Rue Publishing
320 South Boston Avenue, Suite 1030
Tulsa, OK 74103
www.LeRuePublishing.com

ISBN: 978-1-7335960-7-7

For BFD

CHAPTER ONE

KATIE

"We're all gonna die!" I whimper, standing naked in my villa's living room, frozen in place as I watch the helicopter hover outside my window. The man with the gun in his hand jumps from the helicopter and rolls through the grass on the lawn stretching between me and the next villa, not caring that he's mussing his expensive-looking suit. Thankfully he rolls away from me; thankfully the windows are tinted; thankfully it's pretty dark outside.

My mind races a mile a minute as I watch him. I have no idea who this guy with the gun is, but things don't look good. I mean, why the motherfuck is a guy with a gun on our island? Heather rented this entire fucking rock. No one else should be here. Wrong island? Like a Bugs Bunny—should have turned left at Albuquerque—situation? With GPS ... no fucking way. There's no way some whack job messed up and came to the wrong island in the Caribbean. I watch as the helicopter lands a little bit further out in an open patch of grass and Suit's friends hop out. I see two more of them, both wearing sports jackets and sporting stubble, all carrying guns like this is some badass hot mafia romance novel.

Fuck. Normally, I love those novels. Not anymore.

Thoughts of the mafia drag my mind to Peter Brown, the gambling asshole from Heather's harem competition. That asswipe got rejected and is currently hiding in the rain forest like a coward because he owes some bad dudes a lotta cash. Are these mafia hotties here for him? They wouldn't fly down here for a measly thirty grand, would they? The helicopter ride alone would cost that? Did he gamble more than that? Shit, shit, fucking shit. I'm struck dumb.

This is so outside my concept of reality. I don't even know what to do. I don't know how to handle it. I'm stark naked in my villa, breasts covered in cum from the most awesome sex of my life, staring at gangsters pouring out of this helicopter like clowns pour out of a clown car. Is this a giant joke? Like, is Heather pulling a prank on me? She has enough cash to do shit like this now that she won the lotto. A parrot squawks in the palm trees as I try to gauge if Heather would try to give me a heart attack for a laugh. Is this retaliation for the puke pod things? Could she pull something like this off so fast? I mean, she is crazier than an outhouse rat. It's a possibility.

But then Suit checks his weapon. He pulls out the magazine, inspects it, pops it back in. He aims and fires into the trees and a red, dead parrot falls to the ground. Holy shitballs! Those guns are real? Those guns are real! I gulp; my stomach shrinks and sinks all the way to my toes. I try to will myself to move my body and hide, but apparently fight or flight is not auto-programmed into my limbs. I'm a buck-naked brunette rag-doll.

Luckily, my guys don't seem to have the same hang up. Alec, my massive, muscled Hispanic pilot, scoops me up around the waist and silently hauls me back to the bedroom. Inside, Kenneth—my brown-haired, Michelin award-winning orgasm king of the kitchen—is just pulling a shirt down over his happy trail. Danny is back in his tennis-pro, Ken doll wannabe clothes already. Kenneth slips on his shoes as Alec pushes me across the room.

"Get in the closet," Alec orders, his voice gruff and angry. "All of you."

Danny comes across the room and walks toward the closet with me. He takes my hand and caresses my face. He spends a moment staring into my eyes with his gorgeous blue blinkers to calm me down—he's fucking insightful for a lying, little baby sometimes—then he leads me into the closet, to all the extra dresses in plastic I ordered for Heather. I kept them in my villa because that girl and her makeup have a way of ruining anything new and beautiful within a five-foot radius. Now those dresses form a ten-foot wall of glittery, shimmery, potential protection. Tears form in my eyes at that thought. Protection? Those dresses are all that's gonna stop Suit and his friends? I'm a dead woman.

Alec shoves me into the clothes like some two-bit whore he's hiding from his wife. Danny stumbles in behind me, still holding my hand. Alec and Kenneth join us, crouching so their heads can't be seen above the hanging bar. And it takes a second before I realize Alec is still naked. Huh. For the first time, I can't enjoy the view. What a fucking depressing last thought. Those glutes should be sending me into a tail-spin. Instead of wishing I could bite down on them for fun, right now I'm considering biting down to muffle the scream that's lodged in my throat.

Next to me, Danny scratches his nose, and just that slight movement makes the plastic on the dresses rustle as loud as that M&M packet in the movie theater that I timed wrong once. The very second the mood music cut out, I ripped and poured. It sounded like a damned rockslide and people turned and glared at me. It was humiliating on so many levels because it was during a Harry Potter movie. People take that shit seriously. Fuck. And that's what Danny rustling the plastic sounds like now.

Kenneth shoots a hand across my torso and grabs Danny's hand to stop the scratching. He and Alec shush Danny. And I know I should be silent. But ... my brain. It's broken. "I need my clothes," I whisper frantically. Because, for some reason, that's what I can focus on. The fact that I'm naked. Kenneth and Danny aren't. So, I shouldn't be. Alec followed me into the living room, so he isn't dressed either, but my mind doesn't really process that. It's reverting to simple things. Simple problems. Like clothes. I reach out to grab something off the hanger to at least cover myself up, but Kenneth's arm clotheslines me smashing into my neck. I gasp. Alec's hand smacks over my lips and I'm forced to gulp.

"Shhh," Kenneth scolds.

Glass smashes in the vicinity of the living room. I swallow hard. Looks like mafia hotties aren't inclined to knock.

My heart starts up as fast as a racehorse; it's out the door and across the island before I take my next breath. So, I crouch naked, heartless, and about to piss myself in the closet while strange men with guns enter my villa.

Alec's hard chest presses against my back. The sexual tingles he normally gives me just turn into scared shivers. I clench my teeth, close my eyes, and cover my face with my hands. Some people have fight mode. Others have flight mode. I've never been in a near-death situation before. Fight or flight? Nope. Apparently, my fucking response is ostrich mode—squeeze my eyes shut then hope for the best.

Danny squeezes my hand. "It's gonna be okay—" there's a *thwack* sound—"ow!" Danny exclaims. "My balls!"

My eyes click open a quarter of an inch, just in time to see Kenneth smack his hand over Danny's mouth as Danny's free hand covers his balls. Kenneth's slightly shorter than Danny, so he has to reach up to block the blond guy's mouth. But he presses Danny back against the wall with such force, with such venom in his brown eyes, that the young tennis coach just freezes and holds still.

Click clack.

We all stop breathing.

I crouch naked and afraid. Stuck in my closet. Listening to the *click clack* of shoes in the living room. Part of me wonders if this is what cows feel like in the slaughterhouse. Do they know the end is near? Do they feel trapped? Just waiting for it? I'm never eating meat again. My entire body heats up and then goes cold and hot and cold and hot. I feel like a toddler toy. On-off. On-off. My nervous system is on the fritz. Because it doesn't know how to process impending death.

My hands clench and I can feel the panic attack creeping up my spine. I don't want to be the one to blow this cover, weak and pathetic as it is. I don't want to be the reason these armed men find us here. I've no idea who they are or what they're doing, but I know men don't jump out of helicopters with guns without intending to use them. That would be stupid—like turning on the grill in the backyard and just leaving it to flame. It would be like heating oil to fry crappie caught in the lake then just letting the pot bubble on the bank. It would be like Heather wearing four-inch heels around her house. You only strap on fuck me heels if you plan to use them. Just like guns. They're weapons with a purpose.

I turn away from Danny, whose mouth is still covered by Kenneth's hand. Danny looks ready to puke and Kenneth looks like he might take Danny out himself. I think that's just his stress reaction to the situation. But still, neither of their faces are helping me. I need calm. I turn a little and raise my eyes to Alec, hoping against hope that he can do something to help me. He's done the near-death thing before, right? I mean, former fighter pilot, craves the rush—he's gotta be better at this than a kinky chef or an almost Olympian, right?

Alec's deep brown eyes dig into me. His gaze is alert but steady. And I cling to his gaze because it grounds me. My free hand reaches backward and digs into his thigh as our eyes build a bridge and say things to one another.

"I don't want this to be it."

"It won't."

"You promise?"

"I'll keep you safe."

We have an entire unspoken conversation wherein my face says "I'm freaking out!" and his frown says, "Calm the fuck down." And then he slowly gestures at his chest, careful not to nudge the plastic-wrapped dresses next to us. My eyes flicker down. I watch how he takes a slow, deliberate inhale. My eyes flicker up as he silently exhales. I mimic him. I try to shut out the world. I try not to focus on anything else. I try to forget Kenneth and Danny beside me. And I zero in on Alec's eyes and his mouth as he breathes calmly. I try to merge with him at that moment.

It almost works. The way a broken window on your car almost works when you duct tape it to the roof. That is to say, I can't fucking do it. A broken window isn't a very good window with fucking grey tape blocking the view—especially when it can't even open. It's just a fucked up broken shard of stabbiness covered in goo on the outside. That's me —goo and all. I end up raking my nails into Alec's thigh. I dig deeper and harder. My body trembles like a leaf, like a guitar chord, like a motherfucking blender.

Of course, that's when the low-level muttering and the rough scratch of shoes enter my bedroom. I can't make out what the gunmen say, but I do hear three distinct voices. Alec clutches me closer as we hear the bedsheets ripped off the bed. A box is kicked over with a *thump*. I hear the screech of a parrot outside as my sliding glass door is slowly opened and someone steps onto my patio.

"Not here," a man's voice growls in a low accent that I can't place.

"They must just have left—the room is smelling of sex." Another mystery stranger speaks in an accent as the drawers in my dresser are opened and shut. I close my eyes again. I squeeze the lids hard.

God in heaven if you get me out of this, I promise—my brain cuts off. I can't think of anything big enough to promise God in exchange for my life. Fuck me. You promise your soul to the devil to get what you want. But what the hell do you promise the deity? Why isn't there a fucking book or movie about what to promise in this damned forsaken moment?

The closet door opens.

People always say when you're in a life ending moment, you see your life flash before your eyes. Some people piss themselves. But no one's ever told me about how you clench your asshole so hard that you can feel it all the way up your spine in that moment where you think you're about to die. My entire body goes rigid.

In contrast, Alec loosens his grip on me. I'm not sure if that means he's ready to shove me out of the closet as a sacrifice or if he's gonna jump out at these guys and try and tackle them. We didn't discuss tactics. Why didn't we discuss tactics? This is poor planning on our part. Instead of whacking Danny in the balls, we should have been discussing tactics. I'm super disappointed in myself. I'm the planner. I should have planned.

Swoosh. The man pushes aside some of the suits on the opposite side of the closet.

The hairs on my neck rise. And I feel like a cat in an alley. I can feel the gaze of the mafia man looking around the closet, even though I can't see him and even though I'm pretty certain he can't see me in my hiding spot.

Because I have to hold perfectly still, suddenly holding still becomes the hardest thing in the entire universe. I curse myself. *Katie Ann. Don't you motherfucking move, you half-wit Okie. You shoe-chewing slice of white bread!* I strain every piece of willpower within me trying not to move. I even try not to breathe.

Time stretches out. Seconds become minutes, become hours, become eons. It is literally 1.3 billion years later when the asshole with the gun leaves and clicks the closet door shut behind him.

No sooner has the lock clicked, then Danny turns to all of us. "I really have to fart."

My mouth drops open. He did not just say that with a gangster/private army dude/hitman on the other side of the door!

"Not funny," Kenneth grumbles in a whisper so low that I half-think I imagine it.

Danny bites his lip. "Not joking," he whispers.

"Well, hold it," Alec orders gruffly. I look at him. He doesn't swing his eyes away from the door, his entire body is still focused on the potential threat outside our tiny space.

"I've been holding it," Danny whimpers, running a hand through his blond hair.

"Just a little longer," Alec instructs.

"Who are they?" I whisper.

He shrugs. "Not military. Cartel?"

Kenneth shakes his head. "Lots of cartel members have met down here before. It didn't look like them from the bathroom window. A suit? No. Cartel go full on bullet-proof vest."

"I think they might be after Peter Brown," I whisper as I hear my bedroom door close. Holy shit. These guys are leaving. We may actually survive the night. My heart is too exhausted to beat happily, it just pitters pathetically, tripping over itself as it slows down. "I mean, he had that huge debt, right? What if there's more that I didn't find out about? What if he promised them more than the thirty grand?" My heart starts to pick up the pace again. If the guys with guns are leaving, where are they going? Heather's out at the pool with the guys. Fuck. Fuck.

Danny bumps my shoulder, and I look over. His face is strained. His shuffling moves one of the dresses and makes a small rustling noise. Just the tiniest brush of plastic. But Alec and Kenneth both turn and glare.

It's an intense few seconds, but nowhere near as tense as when Gunmetal George inspected the closet. The tension is only broken when a loud, whoopee-cushion worthy squeak erupts.

Danny's face turns tomato red. My hands fly to cover my nose and mouth. Luckily, this doesn't seem to be one of those rotten egg, sulfur-mountain kinda farts. It's just a goddamned bullfrog. Kenneth reaches out to smack Danny, but Alec holds up a hand. We all stop and look to him for direction. He closes his hand until a single finger is raised. And he points at the door.

And suddenly, I'm wishing Danny's ass was the silent-but-deadly type instead of a butt trumpet. Because the handle on the closet door turns.

CHAPTER TWO

HEATHER

I *love sex by the pool. It's all chill, watching the water. And I can climb into the water and wipe down after. Bonus,* I think as I pop up and down on BJ's dick like I'm riding a pogo stick. BJ's dick definitely isn't the biggest of the guys, but his hips are narrow and good for riding. And he likes it when I scratch down his pecs, unlike some of these weak fuckers. Maybe it's the New Yorker in him. Stubborn. Anthony Drake is one of those weaker bitch boys. I hope that slimy asshole gets eaten by sharks. Selling my story to some online trash dump. He motherfucking deserves to be ripped limb from limb—I hit a good spot in my riding and lean into it, trying to wipe Drake from my mind and focus on the pulsing pleasure inside me. The guys are giving me 'forget all your troubles' sex after the three 'forget all your troubles' cocktails they made me. They're fucking thought-ful, my harem wannabes. Booze and orgasms. The perfect forget-an-asshole combo.

I can still taste the mojito on my tongue, and the ocean breeze brings in a delicious combo of salt and chlorine. I'm pretty sure those tastes and scents will be aphrodisiacs for me forever, now. When I'm eighty, sitting in my rocking chair, I'm gonna think back on the days I fucked my harem by the pool on the Spanish tile patio. There are landscape spotlights shooting up through the trees around us, lighting up the night and the pool is a pulse of colored lights beneath the water. Everything together makes me feel like I'm a fucking movie star right now. I bet movie stars have orgies like this. But probably not as good. They don't have guys competing to give them orgasms, competing for a spot in their harem. I'm pretty sure my sex is better. I'm a little smug about that.

I stop popping and start grinding, grabbing the top of BJ's black hair and yanking. His blue eyes widen, but he takes it with a grin.

"Yeah, baby, make yourself come."

I try. But BJ's dick isn't quite enough. It's just a little too thin. I look up. Andrew's on a lounge chair, stroking himself over his swimsuit, casually watching as he sips on bourbon. Jeremiah's downing another shot of tequila—he loves the stuff—as he strokes his staff by the bar. He sets down the shot glass with a thump and wipes his hand across his beard. I'm not a huge fan of beards, but his is just right, long enough to be soft, short enough not to be like a fucking tumbleweed clinging to his face. His brown hair sweeps across his eyes, and he gives a gap-toothed grin when he sees me watching. He licks his lips and then lifts his free hand like a V, wiggling his tongue between his fingers in the universal pussy licking sign. It's a decent offer, he's but not what I want right now.

I glance over at the twins as I sit back and ride a little

harder, my toes curling into the deck tiles. All the guys love it when my tits bounce. Hell, even I love it. The sensation of them jiggling up and down makes me feel wanton. I fucking love letting go.

I watch the twins as I do. Rubin and Reval are naked and they have the bodies of fucking gods. They've got huge biceps lined with veins I love to trace. Their long, thick fingers are a bonus, too. Their abs are chiseled perfection topped by pecs with perky dark nipples. I'm not normally a nipple sucker—but for them, I make an exception. R&R also have these chiseled, beyond amazing square jaw lines. I mean ... it's crazy hot. And their eyes. Fucking puppy dogs would kill for eyes like those. They slope down in this perfect pouty, give-it-to-me way that makes me just want to say "yes." (And then YES! YES! YES!)

The twins watch me ride as they jerk themselves and I wave them over. "Come join in, guys, my titties need some tongue." As usual, they jump at the command. The twins are always up for anything sexual. I watch them walk over. Damn. You'd think abs would get old. But they don't. They fucking don't. Just watching them makes BJ's dick get a bit more soaked. The twins are so fine. I love their long eyelashes. Gah! Everything about them revs me up. R&R— my Russian nesting dolls. They like to be inside other guys just as much as they like getting inside me, which can be hot to watch. There is a bit of a language barrier sometimes. But ... I'm not sure I want to knock them out of the harem yet. Their bedside manner definitely makes up for the lack of manners in other areas.

The twins put pool towels under their knees as they kneel beside me. I can't blame them, the pool deck isn't exactly soft. Which is why I made BJ take bottom. I think about asking if I'm hurting his back, but then he sticks a finger in my ass.

"Yeah, take it," BJ's Brooklyn accent spurs me on.

Sensation shoots all the way up my spine.

"Ohh," I moan as he twists his finger. He didn't lube up, so the sensation is a little sharp. But I like a little bit of rough. I like to ride that edge. I sink down deeper on his finger, letting that little spike of pain mingle with my pleasure. *Mmm.*

I figure BJ must not be too bothered by the hard tile floor if he's thinking dirty like that. I start to writhe on him again, my breasts flopping as I grind harder. I love being on top. I love telling these fuckers what to do. I love that buzzing energy in my pussy that makes my senses light up.

I glance over at Jeremiah Bible, who's moved over to the "pool bag" we keep full of swimming supplies. And by swimming supplies, I mean the boxes of condoms, lube, and sexy swim time toys I need to keep a group of guys entertained. Jeremiah tosses aside a rubber duck vibrator, a triple stimulator, and the giant rope of silicone anal beads. (That right there is a party toy. There is a main line with at least four sets of beads coming up off it. Everybody gets to play.) He finds what he's looking for and comes up holding a bottle of lube in his hand the way a little boy clutches his prize toy car. He's not the prettiest guy. But something about him is homey. Maybe because he grew up all backwoods. Some of these other fuckers are so ... prim. Sometimes you just need a down-home boy. I nod at Jeremiah, signaling he needs to lube up. He tosses on a condom, then pops the lid on that lube tube and starts squirting jelly onto his staff fast as can be.

The twins lean in like synchronized sex machines. Their tongues lave my nipples and my rhythm falters. "Mmm," is all I can get out. They alternate flicks. I have no fucking idea how they can time it so well, but it's perfect. Quick little flicks. One tongue then another. It never gets to be too much. My nipples can get oversensitive during sex, but never with them. They tease until the sensations over-whelm me.

"Clit," I order. Again my sexpot twins respond. They each reach a hand down and start rubbing a finger sideways in opposite directions. Their fingers slide past one another's. My neck starts to roll. And Jeremiah hasn't even joined in yet. He's behind me, but he's waiting until I give him the go-ahead.

I rake my nails down BJ's chest and lean toward him, forcing the twins' mouths to back away. I yank his head up for a kiss and then break it to say, "Jeremiah." BJ's finger slips out of my ass and I groan as Jeremiah fills that void. It's intense. Maybe as intense as the time I saw that coyote, the night I was stumbling home from a drunken bonfire. My heart certainly feels like it's pounding as hard as that night. But nothing about that coyote made my nipples pebble. It might have made my thighs quiver, but never with the expectation of pleasure. It might rank the same on the inten-sity scale, but damn, this intensity is leading me to a chart-topping orgasm. Not many things in life do that to you. Bring intensity and pleasure together. Orgies are one of the few.

With the added sensation, BJ's dick isn't lacking anymore. I use my hands to brace myself on the pool tiles. "Clit!" I order the twins as Jeremiah pushes in another inch. Their fingers saw back and forth faster and bring me back to the brink.

As my body starts to shudder, my eyes seek out Andrew. He only participates in group sex if I absolutely make him. But alone, he's a beast between the sheets. He uses all those premed anatomy classes to his benefit. He knows where it's at. And he's thoughtful, too. Far more than my loser of an ex-husband.

Andrew's in the final three for sure. He knows it. I know it. Even as I fuck other guys, I seek him out. Andrew might not be big on participation. He likes to watch, however. His eyes lock onto mine and he commands, "Say it, Heather."

Normally, I like giving the orders. But not with Andrew. For some reason, it is so fucking hot when Andrew tells me what to do during sex. Especially when he's not even touching me.

The twins' fingers change to circles and pleasure shoots throughout my body. But I don't close my eyes. Because Andrew wants to hear his words. My gaze stays locked on him as my entire body convulses and I say, "You mother-fucking made me come, Andrew!"

Before my eyelids flutter closed, he gets the damned cutest cocky grin on his face. When I do close my eyes, I reach my hands up and shove the twins' faces back onto my breasts. They bite at my nipples, intensifying the sensation. And I almost bliss out into a second mind-numbing orgasm.

But some motherfucking server ruins it by knocking over a table. I'm startled out of my orgasm. Didn't Katie tell the damned staff about us? We've been here for a damn week and a half, almost two! Don't fucking interrupt! My eyes shoot open and my lips part. I'm ready to spit fire at whoever just cut off my O.

But as I look across the pool courtyard, I see it's not a staff member. There are two tall guys standing by the arched entryway to the pool. I might have thought that they were replacement harem members. Consolation prizes from Katie for picking out some goddamned slime-balls. But no. They aren't consolation prizes. I can tell because they hold guns pointed right at us.

My asshole tightens around Jeremiah's dick. And not in a good way. He stops moving. And so do I.

The twins' mouths pop off my breasts and they turn to look at what's causing the hang up.

One of the armed men—the one wearing a suit, with reddish brown hair—smiles at them and says in a broken accent, "So, this is why you do not call us, Reval? Rubin?"

Before I can think, my hand's lashed out and smacked the right-side twin across the face.

That's a mistake. Because, suddenly, the guy in the suit is right in front of me, his gun barrel aimed at my chest.

CHAPTER THREE

KATIE

Gunmetal George is back, his voice calling out, "Did you hear that?" as he stomps into the closet.

This time my eyes are open when he comes in, and I see the gun enter the closet first. Keeping my eyes open was a mistake. Because now I can't close them. All I can do is stare at the barrel as the man holding it violently shoves aside the extra suit jackets I have hanging on the opposite rack.

Just as I'm certain I'm about to join the pathetic, piss-your-pants-scared league of losers, another guy calls out from the other side of the villa in a thick accent, "Look at here! There must be six boxes full of sexy lube!"

The man in the closet turns. And I notice his face for the first time. He's massive. His shoulders alone are bigger than my face. He has a long Roman nose, the kind with a bump in it. He's got dark hair with frosted tips that Heather would hate, and I can see his muscles straining his shirt under his formal jacket. My brain weighs the possibilities, trying to calculate if Alec could take him down. But before I finish my mental assessment, Gunmetal George calls out in a deep, rumbling, undefinable European accent, "No way! You are serious? I thought the article was full of bull. The sexy times are true?" He strides out of the closet, slamming the door behind him. Apparently, boxes of lube are something he needs to verify for himself.

Oh my stars in heaven. I have never been more thankful for Heather's ass sex proclivities. Thank you god of the back door. And to the person who invented lube—please appear in a dream and tell me your name. I'll build a shrine to you. I sag against Alec's chest. His arms wrap around me slowly, careful not to rustle the plastic. Near the wall, one of Kenneth's hands reaches out and strokes down my arm, comforting me as my knees shake in relief.

Danny's arms fly around all of us, plastic noises be damned, enveloping us in a group hug. "Fucking sorry, guys," he whispers.

"I'd punch you in the sac if I didn't think it would make you yelp right now and call that motherfucker back in here," Kenneth growls.

"Shut up," Alec orders. His voice brooks no argument. And despite the fact that he's full-on naked, or maybe because of the fact that he's full-on naked and has scars from two bullet wounds on one side of his torso, he radiates authority. Kenneth and Danny shut the fuck up like naughty little children do when Daddy says, "Five, four..."

Alec pushes Danny back and unwinds the tennis pro's arms from around us all. Alec shoves through the gowns and puts his ear to the door, right by the hinge. When the tension releases from his body, I know what he's gonna say before he says it. He turns to us, "They're gone."

"Thank fuck." Kenneth leaves our cramped hiding space as Alec moves sideways and yanks on the racks of clothing on the other side of the room. Alec finds a suit that's close enough to his size and starts to pull on the pants sans underwear.

Danny wraps his arm around my waist and leads me out to the middle of the closet. I just let him. The touch feels good right now. It proves to me that I'm still alive. It helps ground me because my mind cannot believe what we just went through. Twice. Danny and I both stare at Alec for a second.

"What are you doing?" Danny asks. "You have clothes in the bedroom."

"If I want to be able to get close enough to take them out, I need to look enough like them to trick them..." Alec trails off as the shirt he tries to pull on doesn't close over his massive pecs. He tosses it to the ground of my closet in disgust and grabs a different one. Same problem.

I might be a little giddy from the fact that we didn't actually bite the bullet. But for some reason the fact that Alec's amazing pecs are too big for a shirt is hilarious to me. I start to giggle. When the third shirt doesn't fit, I have to smack my hands over my lips so that I do not full-on belly laugh and end up calling those scary armed men back over here.

Alec just rolls his eyes at me and tells me to get dressed. I go to turn the knob to exit the closet and find something reasonable to wear, but Danny grabs my hand and stops me. "There could still be someone out there. They could be in the hall outside your bedroom. They could still be going through boxes in your living room. Or they could be just outside. There could be a guard at the door ..."

My hand freezes on the doorknob. I release it slowly, blinking like a dumb-ass koala at the zoo. *God, Katie.* My survival instincts suck. Another imperfection my mother could critique. I shake off the image of her that comes to mind. Thinking of her might make me cry. And not out of resentment for once. Fuck. Focus. Focus.

I glance around the closet. It has some of my business suits. And those skirts are way too fucking tight for any run-for-your-life scenario. Because, apparently, I was an idiot who didn't plan to be attacked by men with guns when I planned a tropical vacation. Note to future self, if such a self gets to exist: always have a run-for-your-life outfit. I need a bad-ass, stretchy black outfit that will help me blend with the shadows and somehow contort my body in ways I've never done as I dodge bullets, Matrix-style. My eyes flick quickly over my clothes. They won't work. But the rest of the space is taken up by Heather's fru-fru dresses or extra outfits for the harem guys. "But ... what am I supposed to wear?" I whisper.

Danny yanks at his shorts, drawing my attention to the fact that he dressed so fast that he's actually gone commando. Why the fuck do I have to be in a life-or-death situation with guys so hot that they're distracting? He brushes his blond hair to the side as he points to the awful collection of Heather's fashion. "We can rip off the sparkly stuff. Just grab one."

I start to protest the utter impracticality of wearing big-boob Heather's clothes. They'll just fall off me. "I can't—"

Alec shushes me as he pulls on a dinner jacket, his abs still deliciously on display. If I thought "Commando Ken" was dreamy, Alec is a walking wet dream. All he needs is a stripper pole and he'll be richer than Heather in no time.

All eyes swivel to me.

"I used to be a stripper," Danny says.

It takes me a minute to realize that I made the comment about Alec out loud. Then it takes another second for me to process what Danny said. I turn to him and smack him on the shoulder. "Liar."

"Shh!" Kenneth reminds me.

Danny rubs his shoulder as if I actually hurt him and I just roll my eyes in response.

"Well ...I could've been a stripper," he says defensively. In all honesty, he could still be a stripper and make a ton of money. But that's beside the point.

Kenneth leans his ear against the closet door for a minute and says, "I think they might be going through more boxes in your living room. Something about strobe lights and cats or something."

"You can hear that?" Danny asks.

"All of my senses are very acute," Kenneth responds. "I have to listen for steam—"

Danny holds up a hand, "Never mind. Okay. You're Superman. Got it. Can I be Batman?"

"How about you just be quiet?" Alec grumbles as he studies the contents of the closet.

Danny mutters under his breath but complies.

Kenneth puts his hands on my waist and guides me towards the gowns as Alec starts yanking apart metal hangers and twisting them into long, pointed skewers. My head turns and I watch Alec as Kenneth starts quietly and quickly rifling through Heather's dress collection. I tilt my head as I try and figure out what our pilot is doing. He bunches twenty or so hangers together, long jagged points roughly aligned. And then he starts to bundle them by wrapping another hanger around them.

Kenneth pulls out a floor-length gown that's not wrapped in plastic—one of Heather's rejects from her debut night here —and then slips it back onto the rack. He grumbles as he sorts through the ridiculous outfits that my BFF insisted we had to bring. Half of them trail the floor and would be totally inappropriate for whatever the hell it is Alec thinks we're gonna do—some MacGyver/James Bond shit or something.

Finally, Kenneth finds a dress that has shoulders and isn't dragging a three-foot train behind me. But it's slutty as fuck. I roll my eyes as I slide it on. It's a dress that I'd never wear in a million years. It's half black satin, half delicate black sheer. A thick black strip of satin crosses horizontally at my neck. But then there's a sheer strip of fabric on the sleeves and bodice of the dress before a three-inch black strip covers my triceps and the essentials on my breasts. My torso is mostly on display with sheer black material. There's another thick strip of black material just below my navel, as though it's the skirt, but nope. A peekaboo, thin strip of sheer material occurs just above the zone of no return. Then a black miniskirt finishes off the dress. Never ever in my entire life—even when Heather was giving me all kinds of drunken dares in high school—did I ever wear dresses this risqué. I try to yank the material to cover my boobs a little better but that just reveals a lot of under boob. I'm damned if I do, damned if I don't. My breasts are still coated in cum, so that's super fun and uncomfortable, too.

Kenneth yanks on the back of my skirt a little (it hardly covers my ass) and then rubs his hand down my side. "You look delicious," he whispers just before we hear a distant thump. It sounds like Gunmetal George and his friend, Suit or whoever, have left the building, shutting the door behind them. Thank fuck. I take a second to appreciate Kenneth's fingers dragging up my side because, well, it feels fucking good to be alive right now. I give into Kenneth's caress for one life-reaffirming moment before I turn back to the others.

"What's the plan?" I ask, now that I'm fairly confident the coast is clear. "How are we gonna warn Heather? How do we tell the staff?"

Kenneth holds up a necklace from underneath his t-shirt. "I've buzzed them."

"What is that?"

He fingers the little black pendant. "It's like a distress beacon. With the kind of people who rent this place ... the staff have to have a couple security measures in place ... for our own safety," he trails off and shakes his head. "We've only ever used it for real once before. Anyway, if this worked, they're already gone. There's a hidden speedboat for the staff."

"Fuck," Danny says. "You couldn't hold off for us to get there?"

"I was pretty sure we were goners," Kenneth responds bluntly.

I close my eyes and take a deep breath, seeking calm. Maybe the staff saved Heather and the guys. Maybe she's okay. The tight feeling in my chest eases a bit.

Kenneth and Danny start to bicker and I turn back to Alec, trying to ignore them. I ask again, "What's the plan?"

Alec doesn't give me a straight answer. He mutters things as he makes the world's largest homemade hanger weapon. Obvious things like, "We need to find out why they're here." And, "No matter why, we need to take them out."

Danny tosses up his hands at Kenneth and walks over to Alec. Danny starts unbending hangers and handing his straightened creations to Alec.

"The helicopter. That's our biggest problem," Alec repeats that line a number of times.

"Why?" Kenneth asks.

"They can either take us away, or shoot us like fish in a barrel," Alec responds.

"You don't fly helicopters?" I ask even though my stomach's already sinking, anticipating his response.

"Nope," Alec grits out.

Fuck. I move, trying to keep busy so the churning in my stomach doesn't turn into upchuck. I bend down and sort through extra men's shoes to see if there's anything that'll fit Alec. If we're gonna have to run for it, we can't go barefoot. It's pure dumb party-planning over-thinking luck that I brought an extra set of men's shoes in every size. I find a size eleven for Alec. He slips on the shiny dress shoes, grumbling about how the shoes aren't good for tracking, or tromping through the forest, or running.

I ignore the man-wailing and focus on my own shoes, since apparently, we're not leaving the closet until we're completely ready to run at the first sign of Gunmetal George. I find a decent set of hiking boots in the back of my closet, but Alec won't let me leave to get socks. So instead, I settle on some Teva sandals I tossed in on a whim. They look rocking with my dress. Sex hair and Teva hippie shoes meet whore-torso. Yup. I'm like one of those awful Walmart weirdo photos.

When Alec's weapon is ready, he slides it up the arm of his suit coat, leaving a dangerous array of tiny spears protruding just beyond his fingertips. He goes to the door of the closet and we line up behind him. Kenneth and I carry stilettos in our hands with spike heels. Danny pulls down a short hanging rod. It's only plastic, but he takes a practice swing behind me and I want to duck because the air swishes over my neck as fast as a fat man trying to beat a food truck line.

Alec leads the way through my villa like a dark scary mother goose—the kind that will peck you to death with her beak. His beak is a bunch of rusty hangers. Honestly, I think if he just punched people, we might be better off. Shivers crawl up and down my spine like spiders, and my head whips every which way. I don't know what the fucking fuck we're gonna do if one of those guys is hiding behind my boxes. For the first time, I curse my over-planning, hoarder self. I gave those gunny assholes so many places to hide.

But we make it to the living room without incident. On the

side table—how did they not grab it?—my cell sits where Alec tossed it.

I rush over to it and unlock it with my fingerprint, determined to warn Heather, eager to call the Caribbean police, a private army, whatever the fuck it takes.

But there's no signal.

Alec reaches his hand for the phone when he sees me stare at it several times. He yanks it away just before I can start madly mashing buttons. Danny comes up behind me and wraps me in a hug. He kisses the back of my head as Alec checks the phone.

"No service," Alec grunts. "They must have jammed the signal."

"Who could do that?" Danny asks, clutching me closer.

Kenneth shakes his head. "We've had cartel meetings do it before. When members of two families meet. Had a couple of government officials jam the signal one time. Obviously, those meetings announced it beforehand and our old manager gave us a heads up, but ... it's possible."

"Is there a jammer on site?" Alec asks.

"Nope."

"Fuck. Then the first target definitely needs to be the helicopter."

"We'll follow your lead," Kenneth nods at Alec.

I'm kind of surprised by how calm he's being right now. Like, literally, I'm so disappointed in myself. I never thought I was totally brave. But I never thought I was such a coward either. If Heather weren't possibly about to go head to head with gunmen, I'd totally say screw the helicopter and let's just hide in my villa forever. We have everything we could ever need. There's lube. And flower tape. Tablecloths I brought in case the ones here were shit ... completely useful stuff.

I remind myself that Heather would never leave me behind. She might not make it five feet to my rescue because she'd mouth off so much, but she'd try for the five feet. I pussy up and make my stupid coward feet shuffle forward as Alec heads toward my front door.

Danny clutches his closet pole like a baseball bat. Kenneth grabs one of my hands and squeezes. He raises a metal-tipped stiletto in the other. I mirror him.

All together, my guys and I step out into the dark, dangerous night.

CHAPTER FOUR

HEATHER

"You're with these fuckers?" I slide off BJ's dick and stand, stepping over him and turning toward the twins. I channel rage at Reval and Rubin, not bothering to look at the man with the gun aimed at my tits, even as he takes a few steps closer, his fancy-looking gun and suit all lit up in playful, rainbow fucking colors from the party lights inside the pool. If I look at him, this will become too real. And I'll get scared. I don't want to get scared. I want to be pissed.

R&R don't answer me. Because they're beta cowards when it comes down to it. Fuck them. Automatic disqualification from the harem if you ruin my orgasms with gunmen. I don't even have to know why.

They stare back at me, apologies leaking from their eyes. I don't give a good goddamn about apologies. Shane Paul ruined the word "sorry" for me long ago. It's an empty fucking lie.

The gunman in the suit clears his throat and speaks over his shoulder to one of his cronies. "Is this her?" He sidesteps a bit to give that other asshole a better view of me.

I narrow my eyes and peer around Suity McGunPants. There, at the edge of the shallow end of the pool, is a guy who looks vaguely familiar. He's tall and slightly balding, with a forehead that would still be abnormally large even without the hair loss. I study him. He's has a bit of a paunch that's been hidden a bit by his jacket. He's also looks a little bit nervous about being here. He's got dishwater-brown hair and a bit of a blob for a nose. He's pretty forgettable, to be honest. Maybe it's just the gun at my chest that makes me hyper aware and makes me think I know him. Or maybe it's just one of those weird moments of déjà vu. But I feel like I've seen Blob before, I just can't quite place him.

Blob takes a few hesitant steps closer and stares at me. He clears his throat and says, "Yes, it is her." His accent makes the words hard to understand. It takes my ears a second to process them and catch up.

"Who?" I ask. "Who the fuck are you? You don't know me!"

Suity taps my chest with the gun. And motherfuckin' adrenaline hits me. I reach up and twist his hand in so hard that he drops the weapon with a howl. Bet he didn't expect that from a bitch he pointed a gun at. *Stupid ass hothead,* I curse him in my mind. *Get your red-headed temper under control. And don't use guns to jab at people like you're a little bitch. Guns are for shooting. You even know that?* I smirk at him. Not that it does a lotta good, because just then, another of Suity's friend walks through the arch. This guy is massive; he has huge football shoulders. As soon as he takes in the scene, he's got his gun trained on me. I glare at him. He looks like Katie's usual type. An asshole with an attitude. I decide to call him Jeremy 2.0.

"Don't move."

He could be a Schwarzenegger impersonator—J2. He's got the voice and build for it. He's got some frosted tips in his hair that are a little unfortunate, though. Too bad he's on the bad guy team. I could totally have fixed those for him. And that little soul patch on his chin. He just needs to shave that shit off. It looks like those little patches of pubic hair women sometimes leave right above their slits. Not cute.

I listen to this guy's command and freeze. Because, unlike Suity, J2 isn't getting close and poking me with his gun like it's a stick. He's got a wide-legged, double-handed, proper shooting stance going on. I let Suity grab his little metal dick back off the ground, glaring at him the whole time.

"I could shoot you dead," Suity threatens.

"You woulda' already done that if it's what you came here to do," I toss back at him.

J2 snickers behind Suity.

I cannot imagine being surrounded by bigger dopes than these ... I make eye contact with Andrew and he shakes his head, discouraging me from continuing to engage. But I can't freaking help myself. If I'm about to die, I'm gonna go down swinging. I'm just so motherfucking glad Katie isn't here right now. First, because she'd freak out, and second, because then I'd be worried about getting her shot. It's tough enough right now. But these are guys. I expect them to man up or duck and cover. I don't feel responsible for them the way I would for her. I'm in such a rage that I don't even care right now. I mean, this is *my* motherfucking island! They're trespassing. And they ruined my forgetting sex. "How the hell did you get on this island?"

Suity doesn't answer. But I have even more questions for him. I don't pause long, I just let the questions roll. Maybe one of them will get a response. At least a facial expression or something that'll give me a clue about what's going on. "Why do you think you know me? What's your beef with me? What's with the guns? If you have a goddamn problem with me, why don't you man up and say it instead of waving a gun in my face? Are you compensating for something?"

Andrew literally slaps a hand over his eyes at that last question. But I just purse my lips and stare at Suity and then at J2. Someone better give me some answers or shoot me. Neither of them moves to do either. Which tells me that these two are low on the totem pole. They're here to threaten, but their dumb brute gazes don't hold answers. And I'm pretty sure I've insulted them enough to shoot me if they were gonna. My momma always pushed back with those guys she cheated on daddy with. Sometimes she shouldn't have and she got smacked around. But there it is. When she pushed back and the guy did nothing, she let him stick around for awhile, knowing she held the reins. But she always pushed back—she had to, in order to see what she was working with. Apparently, I'm working with apes who carry guns.

My gaze shifts over to R&R again. I stare those beta bitches down. "What the hell is going on?"

Reval chews on his lip. That's about the only time I can tell the fuckers apart. That's his nervous tell. He usually does it right before he gets reamed in the ass. I hold eye contact until he submits.

He opens his mouth and words come spilling out. "You weren't supposed to be there. It was supposed to be a clean buy. He was supposed to get all the tickets."

I scrunch my eyebrows. What he's saying doesn't really make sense. And yet, somehow, a little part of my brain is saying it does. I take a second trying to string together crazy boy's words. The thing I latch onto is ticket. The only ticket I've bought recently was that lotto ticket. Best pissed-off mood I ever had. The guy in front of me was holding up the motherfucking line. Wearing a baseball cap and trying to buy a zillion tickets so I couldn't get my goddamn Power-ade. He was taking forever! I literally walked up, hip checked him, smacked down the cash for the Powerade, scooped up a freshly printed ticket, tossing an extra two bucks on the counter. I'd flipped off the dickhead in the hat and walked out.

I zero back in on Blob. I didn't notice a paunch that day, but I think he was wearing a jacket then, too. I study his face. His hunched posture. His duck-footed stance. Recognition dawns. He was the idiot at the gas station buying all those lotto tickets.

"You took our father's ticket," Rubin says slowly. His eyes don't quite meet mine.

"It wasn't your father's ticket, I paid for it," I respond.

"It was printed for me, yet you took," Blob accuses.

Suity shakes his gun and his head, *tsk*ing at me.

"Fuck you," I jerk my chin at Blob and again at Suity. What

the hell? "Not every ticket is yours. You can't buy every goddamned ticket."

"Actually," Reval shrugs. "That's exactly what Boris was supposed to do."

My jaw drops. "But that's cheating!" Motherfucking brilliant. But who has the cash to buy every goddamned ticket?

I eye R&R and their little posse. It looks like the answer is the Russian mafia.

CHAPTER FIVE

KATIE

W e carefully edge around the corner of my villa. The adrenaline is pumping through my veins, urging me to go as fast as possible. I'm ready to race down the path and save Heather from these motherfucking crazies. How? I dunno. Startling them to death is about the best I can come up with. I wish an awkward wave was as deadly in real life as it is for my social life. Dammit. I stare down the path, bleakly anticipating my own suckiness.

But Alec doesn't go down the path toward the pool, he turns and heads through the grass, straight toward the helicopter.

I almost mess everything up. I almost yell after him. I almost ask, "What the hell are you doing?"

But I spot the silhouette leaning against the helicopter. At first, the man's nearly impossible to see given the dark shadows. It's only the fact that the moon peeks out from behind the cloud and basically points right fucking at him, that I see him at all. One gangster stayed behind.

We crouch in the flowery bushes next to my villa and the smell is awful. It's like my grandmother's potpourri obsession come to life. I have to hold my breath as I spy on the bad guy. He has on jeans and a tan sports jacket and he's picking at his fingernails with a pocket knife that glints in the moonlight.

Watching him sparks some part of me that I've never in my life experienced before. This little rage monster snarls in my head and wants to shove that knife right between his ribs for coming here and scaring me, for searching my villa, and making me fear for my life. My mother would be horrified I'm having such thoughts. But I bet some ancestor in the sky is saying, "Yee haw! Git 'em!" or maybe some even more primitive ancestor is beating his chest with an, "Oogh." Kill or be killed. My belated fight instinct kicks in and I welcome it to the party. But just as soon as it appears, it vanishes like sand between my fingers. Which figures. Because while I might daydream about aggression, I am just not that girl.

Alec stares at the gangster for a minute, sizing him up before turning to us and giving some kind of fucking hand signal. What the hell? Are we in a cop show? Is this baseball? Are we speaking sign language now? I don't know what the hell his hand signal means. It looks like he's doing a messed up interpretive dance or a really bad robot, maybe. But for some reason, Kenneth and Danny both nod. What the fuck? My eyes flicker over to them, but they both sneak back the way we came without another word. Did they actually understand? Am I missing something? Is there a class in high school that teaches this shit? Or ... wait ... no, there's gotta be some dumb guy comedy movie that has this in it. And like every guy who memorizes movie quotes and wastes his brain space on useless shit, this hand signal is one of those things that all guys just "know." That's gotta be it.

Alec turns away without confirming that I understand his little finger-pointing, elbow-flapping hand signals. He goes back to staring at the bad guy for another second. I shake my head and roll my eyes and decide to just follow along behind Alec. Hopefully I don't screw up the plan of the only person in our little quad that knows anything about attacking others.

Suddenly, Alec leaves our bush. Not running, not stealthy. He just stands up and walks. Alec marches right toward the motherfucker in the sports coat leaning on the helicopter. What in the holy name of hell? *This* is his plan! Suddenly I'm rethinking his intelligence. Because this plan seems a few peas short of a casserole.

My choices are to stand where I am or follow the fathead with the homemade hanger weapon. My brain must be fried because I choose to follow the fucktard. I don't know why. I could justify it by saying that I think he'll take most of the bullets ... but I don't really know if that logic is true. My feet just move.

I run like a maniac to keep up with Alec, but it does no good. The guy leaning on the chopper sees us and swings around. He flips his knife shut and reaches for that nice, shiny firearm on his hip. And does he point his weapon at the big, hulking man striding toward him? Nope. He points his gun right at me.

Dammit! I freeze. Alec doesn't. I stick my hands in the air when Sports Coat waves his gun.

"Don't move," Sports Coat barks at me.

Alec turns to look at me, like he's surprised I'm there. In fact, his eyebrows lower like he's pissed to see I followed him.

We have another of those silent conversations, only this time he's scolding me instead of comforting me.

Sports Coat approaches behind Alec, "I've got her covered."

Guess Alec's disguise is working well enough, then.

When Sports Coat gets within Alec's reach, I gulp, not sure what's gonna happen next. Apparently, gulping is the signal for attack. Alec swings his arm at the stranger; the arm that's been reinforced with tiny hanger daggers. He whacks Sports Coat right in the neck. The other man stumbles backward and Alec moves immediately to disarm the other man.

Sports Coat squeals like a piglet when Alec touches his hand. They scuffle. I bite my lip, unsure what to do as the damn moon closes her eye and leaves us back in a mess of shadows. I lean forward a bit, then step back, then take half a step forward. It's like second grade all over again, trying to jump into the damn ropes for double dutch. I'm trying to time jumping into the fight so I actually help. Only, I don't know when that might be.

My moment finally comes when I see Alec kick the gun away. Then I know exactly what to do. I beeline it for that motherfucker. I snatch it up.

"I have his gun," I call out. But Alec doesn't turn to acknowledge me; he's busy groaning after Sports Coat's nut shot.

I call out a little louder. "I don't think you heard me. I got his gun! You can stop now."

Alec just grunts and slams Sports Coat's head into the grass. They roll around on the ground like two monkeys.

"If you just back the fuck off, I can point the gun at him," I grouse as I click the safety off the gun and train it away from them. Like any good Oklahoma girl, I learned to shoot young. My daddy took me when I was growing up. But I haven't touched a gun in years. And so I mentally review the steps when suddenly a gunshot goes off. I stare at the gun in my hand. Did I accidentally ...?

I hear bones crack. Sports Coat howls.

Alec grunts and another small gun flies through the air. "Correction," Alec grates out. "You got *a* gun."

Well, smack me in the face and call me stupid. Of course, he had two guns. What self-respecting bad guy wouldn't? My cheeks burn red as I run across the grass and scoop up a small revolver. I guess my role here is more weapons collector than anything. Shortly after gun number two, Alec tosses the pocket knife my way. I slide that onto the neck-line of my dress because I literally have nowhere else to put it.

I'm just adding a set of brass knuckles to my weapon collection when Kenneth and Danny make it around the building and up to us.

"Damn," I poke fun. "Stop to take a shit?"

Danny turns red.

I shake my head. "Never mind. Don't answer." I look at Kenneth and ask, "Know how to shoot a gun?"

We turn to watch Alec put Sports Coat in a headlock.

Kenneth cocks his head and asks, "He's still not out? I thought you'd have knocked him out by now."

Alec snarls, "You wanna come down here and choke him out instead?" Alec's face is turning red with the effort of holding Sports Coat down.

"Nope I'm good," Kenneth replies.

There's an awkward period of silence where Alec squeezes tighter, Sports Coat flails and wheezes, and Danny, Kenneth, and I just stare off into the distance ... then at each other ... then off into the distance ... waiting. It takes a lot longer than I expect for Sports Coat to go limp.

Alec sighs and sits back in the grass, recovering.

Danny leans over the stranger. "He's still breathing."

Alec nods. "He's just passed out."

I nod. "Alright then. So, we need to tie him up, maybe?"

Alec nods.

Finally! Something I can do. "I've got jute rope back in my villa, I'll just go run and..." I'm moving and trailing off.

"Katie!" Alec's voice stops me. He holds out a hand. "Gimme a gun."

I trot back and hand him one.

He raises a brow when I keep the other.

"Hey, I know how to shoot. Targets at least."

He clamps his lips together to suppress a smile. "Alright.

You can keep it. But give those bozos the knife and the knuckles."

I pass out the other weapons and then head back down the dip in the grass toward my villa. Someone follows, but I don't look back. I just take comfort in the warm presence guarding me.

I get into my villa and head over to the unused fireplace. That's where I put the boxes with flower tape, twine, all kinds of random supplies. I open the flaps of one box and start to dig in. "It should be in one of these three boxes," I say.

I see Kenneth grab a box out of the corner of my eye. He starts digging. But he doesn't get very far before he stops and rubs his chin. "Um ... why do you have cat litter in here?"

I look up from where the ribbon wheels I'm tossing aside. "Don't you use those in your kitchen?"

"Um. No."

"Oh, it's great for spills. It's crazy absorbent. It's got these crystals that just suck up all the ..." I trail off at Kenneth's disbelieving look.

"Don't *ever* bring that stuff in my kitchen."

"Okay, geez. I just like to be prepared."

Kenneth just gives me a disbelieving head shake before he reaches into his box and pulls out a roll of twine.

"Jackpot!" I give him a high five with my free hand and we make our way back outside, me in front, holding my gun down and creeping sideways like they do in cop shows. "So ... know how to tie people up?"

Kenneth grins and slides closer to me. "Katie, if you want me to truss you up sometime, just ask."

I giggle awkwardly but a little shiver runs down my spine. I'm sure if Kenneth were to do that to me, he'd be amazing at it. "I meant, like, bad guys." I try to steer the topic toward the pressing issue at hand.

But Kenneth slaps my ass and says, "I'm so glad I didn't die tonight."

"Me too."

"I definitely don't want to die before I tap that again."

I laugh. It's not poetry, but it works.

We rejoin Alec and Danny and try to determine the best way to tie up Sports Coat. In the end, we decide to go full cocoon. We wrap him shoulders to feet in skinny brown twine.

Once the bad guy is secure and I'm standing over him with my gun pointed at him like I'm some badass who knows what she's doing, Alec slides open the door to the helicopter. He hops in and takes a look around. He tries the radio, but it's all static.

"Dammit. Bet the mountain blocks the radio signal," he gestures over at the rise that leads up to the waterfall. He gives up on sending a distress signal and searches under the seats, pulling open the luggage compartment. But the thing is empty. Not a scrap of paper with notes on what they're doing or anything.

"Six seater," he calls out. "So we should assume it was full."

"But, if it was full, then they couldn't take anyone back with them," I protest.

Alec lifts a shoulder. "Not alive. But that luggage compartment's empty."

I tremble at the implication. Next to me, Danny swallows hard. The only reason I could think these guys would land here and want to bring back a body is because they've been wronged. Dammit all, Peter Brown! It kinda makes me want to find him and kick him myself. He's the fucking ass-teroid who's caused our own personal apocalypse.

"So, if we have one, then there are five more out there," Danny shakes his head. "Damn."

Alec hops down onto the grass and turns to stare up at the chopper, examining it. "Best way to make sure a chopper can't fly is to take out the tail rotor." He eyes it.

Danny studies it. "I could do that, hit rocks at it or something."

Alec shakes his head. "Too loud. Same with the guns. If we shoot it, this guy—"

"Sports Coat," I supply.

"What?"

Apparently, I've derailed his train of thought.

"Heather and I like to come up with nicknames for people we don't know. So, we can tell who we're talking about. So, we'll say, like, remember Jellybean at the mall?"

"Jellybean?"

"The guy had bright green hair."

"So, your nicknames are unoriginal and all about appearance?" Danny asks.

"Hey!"

"I say Katie's new nickname is Nipples," Danny says.

Kenneth nods. "Done."

My fingers clench and I nearly pull the trigger. "Fuck you, Ken doll."

Danny's eyes widen and dance with mirth. "I like it. Sex symbol. But Ken doll and Kenneth could be confusing. What should we call him? Shorty?"

Kenneth cocks his head and stares at Danny. "Maybe you should be called Quickie based on how fast you—"

Alec's nostrils flare and he pinches the bridge of his nose. "Shut up and focus!" Alec turns to Kenneth. "Do you know where the nearest garden hose is? Where is the closest grounds keeper shed?"

"Katie's villa is the farthest out," Kenneth shakes his head. "There's no way we be able to get to anything without crossing paths with the rest of those creeps."

"Fuck."

"A hose? To suction out the gas?" I ask.

Alec nods and I stare up at the big, mean, flying monster that spit six assholes down on us and consider how I might be able to break it. I lick my lips as I ponder the options. And the event-planning, contingency awareness, end-of-the-world worrywart part of my brain lights up. I turn to Kenneth, a self-satisfied smile stretching across my face as I ask, "What if we soak up the gas ... with cat litter?"

I try not to do a smug happy dance as the guys pour cat litter into the gas tank. But I fail. I totally shoulder shimmy with a gun still in my hand.

Once that's done, we have to decide what we want to do next. Should we go down to the pool and try a rescue mission? Or should we go into the forest and try to snag Peter Brown?

"They'll come back to check on Sports Coat eventually," Kenneth gestures at our prisoner, who's still out cold. I give him a shoulder bump for embracing the nickname and he smiles at me and rolls his eyes. Ugh—he's got the best smile. It transforms his face. We share a moment before we both turn back to the discussion at hand.

"But, we might need a bargaining chip," Danny argues. "We go in now, then we'll be empty-handed."

Alec nods. "That or, at least, we need a distraction. If we can get Peter Brown and get back down here quickly, maybe two of us bring him in while the other two sneak in through the back with the guns. If we're coming from behind ... we might have a shot."

Kenneth plays devil's advocate. "But, if Heather and her harem are still on the island and they didn't leave with the staff, they could need us now."

That thought alone has me dancing on my tiptoes with anxiety. Shit. What do we do?

"We can't know either way for sure unless we walk down there right now." Alec shrugs.

Kenneth toes Sports Coat. "What if we go for Brown and also try to get this asswipe to talk when he wakes up? I mean, then maybe we could get some more intel on their plan and stuff."

Alec grinds his teeth together in thought. It's the first non-hot, mildly annoying habit I've seen from him.

Danny sighs, "I wish they had fucking walkie talkies so we could hear their plans."

"This is real life, not some movie, dimrod," Kenneth rolls his eyes.

"I know that! I can still wish—"

Kenneth opens his mouth to get chippy.

"Don't!" I hold up a hand. "Just ... don't. We need to think this through." All the guys turn and look at me. And suddenly it feels like I've been tossed inside a pressure cooker. "Whoa. Um, why are you all staring at me?"

"Heather's your friend," Alec says. "What do you think we should do?"

Oh crap. Me? He wants to know what I think? I'm with Danny. I'm all for wishful thinking. I don't want this reality. I don't want to be here in this moment. I don't want this weight in my chest, like the damned ghost of Jacob Marley —wrapped in chains—is suddenly possessing me. I want to skip to the end and miss the scary bits and the life lessons. I just want it to be Merry Christmas and happily ever after and all that. My mind goes back and forth like a swing in a windstorm. Do we take the bad guys on now, head on? Or do we wait and try to trick them?

I pick at my hair and avoid their eyes. I'm not qualified to choose. What if I make the wrong choice? What if Heather's down there? What if I make the wrong choice and she dies? What if I make the wrong choice and one of my guys dies? Or what if someone gets hurt? What if they hate me for it? I start breathing harder. I can't …

Alec steps up to me, right into my bubble. We're toe to toe and I can feel the heat radiating from his skin. I can see the scratches weeping on his chest, the bruises blooming. "Katie, choose."

"I can't—"

"Choose or I'll kill him." Alec gestures at Sports Coat.

"What!?"

"Prisoners are usually more trouble than they're worth," Alec shrugs. "But you choose. What do you want? You have five seconds."

My skull's an inferno. This isn't happening! He can't be serious. He's joking, right?

Alec cocks his gun. He takes a step closer to Sports Coat. "Pool or waterfall?" He takes aim.

Panic clouds my thoughts and I try to swat it away. I can't let him! He can't! We—I—I blurt out the first thing I can. "Waterfall!"

Alec slowly moves his gun away from Sports Coat. He smiles at me. "Good job."

I fall to my knees on the grass. "I can't believe you were gonna kill him." I'm so angry and sick to my stomach right now. I thought I knew him. What the fuck?

"I wasn't gonna kill him," Alec puts the safety back on his gun and tucks it into his waistband. "I just wanted to know what you thought. Not what you thought we wanted to hear. But what you, Katie, on an instinctual level, thought was the right choice."

Tears come to my eyes. And that panic that's been seething inside me finally pushes it's way through my stomach and out my lips. I puke on the grass.

Alec comes to put an arm around me, but I shove him off. "Fuck you and your life lessons."

He doesn't say anything in response to that. He just stands, hands Kenneth his gun, and slings Sports Coat over his shoulder. "I'll see you at the waterfall." He walks off.

Danny scoops me into his arm and places a gentle kiss on my forehead. He doesn't say anything, which is nice. He just carries me away from my villa and toward the path that leads up the mountain. Kenneth follows, guarding our rear.

I slump in Danny's arms as the adrenaline leaves me. He carries me, but it doesn't seem to slow him down. He and Kenneth catch up with Alec pretty quickly. I'm almost asleep when I hear screaming. Female screaming. The shrill sounds of a voice I know all too well.

I scramble out of Danny's arms and fall to my knees on the

path. But I don't even care. I stand and turn; we all turn to look back in the direction of the villas. We can't see them anymore. Trees block the view. But there's one more loud screech.

My hand goes over my heart. No! Heather!

CHAPTER SIX

I scream for all I'm worth. Then I yell at those stupid twins. "You asshole motherfuckers! Why the hell are you even here, huh? Did they send you?"

The twins have the good sense to look ashamed. As they should. They're damn lucky I didn't pick up Suity McGunpants' weapon when I had the chance or they might be full of holes right now. My lip twitches. If there's one thing I can't stand since Shane Paul, it's a lying cheater. And now, I'm looking at two of them. Somehow, these jerkoffs weaseled their way onto the harem list and onto my plane, all because of that lotto ticket and some male sense of entitlement. I should have hired bodyguards like Katie suggested when she planned this thing. Fuck. I'd thought she was being overprotective, paranoid about guys getting too obsessed with me or desperate for my money. I hadn't thought she'd be right.

Dammit. Katie's paranoia: 1. My idiotic ass: 0.

I'm so pissed I got sucked in by R&R. I was even considering letting them make the final cut at one point, despite the fact that they never smile, congratulate me when I get out of the shower like it's some accomplishment (which is weird and annoying), and even despite the fact they often call me "girl" which incites my southern womanhood's ire to no end. Anger bites at my insides. My fingers flex, frustrated by my inability to wring their stupid Russian necks. Well, if I can't kill them ... I'll at least fucking tell them what I think of them. "You spineless, brainless cocksuckers! You came all the way out here to trick a woman outta her money?"

"Our money," Blob interjects.

I ignore him, watching Rubin as he stands, his dick a little limp worm just like him, and backs away. I take a step closer. No fucking way. He's not getting out of answering for this. "What the hell was with the mediocre sex? You think I'd pay you out like whores?!"

That does it. That insult finally sparks a little bit of fire in Rubin's eyes as he mentally translates what I've said. "We are not that. We are not shlyukha."

"Shlooka? That mean whore? If you're fucking me to get my money—yeah you are." I take a step closer to Rubin, ignoring Suity and his gun. My eyes burn into this asshole's.

Rubin takes a step forward, like he's gonna put his motherfucking hands on me. *Do it, asshole. I dare you.* I step forward again.

Andrew calls out, "Heather, maybe now's not the best—"

"Shut it!" I hold up a hand to dismiss him like I did Blob, but somehow that feels wrong. Snapping at him cuts me inside and guilt wells up. I'm not actually mad at Andrew. And he's just trying to calm me down so I don't get shot to bits. I have to take a deep breath and calm myself. I look away from Rubin and over at Andrew's soft brown eyes. I bite my lip and say, "Sorry."

He gives me a sad half-smile and holds out his arms.

Somehow that gesture breaks the spell I'm under. It snaps my anger in half and lets me walk away. Rubin's still standing there, looking like an idiot, as I leave him and walk across the pool tiles to Andrew. For some reason, Suity and Blob let me. Maybe because they've decided to jibber jabber with Reval in Russian. I can't tell if they're fighting or if that's just what Russian sounds like. But none of them look happy. Good.

J2 stands a bit apart from the others. He keeps his gun trained on me, like the asshole he is, but he lets me walk without protest.

I glance over at BJ and Jeremy, who are squatting on the pool tiles, having their own whispered conversation, their eyes on J2. I can't tell what they're thinking, but Jeremy swallows hard, so I'm pretty sure they're feeling the same body-ache inducing fear that I am, even if theirs isn't over-laid with rage. BJ's fist clenches and that gives me a little surge of pride. He should be angry. R&R betrayed all of us.

When I reach Andrew, I sink onto the lounge chair in front of him, moving his legs aside to make space. Andrew pulls me onto his lap. He's the only one of us not naked. He's still wearing his swimsuit, and it's a silly swimsuit. It's got floating hot dogs all over it. I stare at it as Andrew wraps his arms around me. I let myself go blank for a minute, just staring at the hot dog pattern, not thinking, not feeling. Betrayal ... can leave you hollow. It's so overwhelming, so all encompassing, so exhausting. You can end up wrung out like a rag. I feel a little like that as I sink into Andrew's arms. Wrung out.

"Hey," he whispers, tracing circles on my hips with his fingertips. "I love how you hit the gun out of that guy's hands. That was hot."

I chuckle. "Yeah?"

"Yup. Only, next time, if you don't mind ... actually grab the gun."

"Then they'd have shot me."

"Not before you tossed the gun to me. I coulda' taken them all down."

"You shoot?"

"Not at all." I can hear Andrew's smile in his voice. I twist around because I have to see it. How can he be so silly and calm in this moment?

Andrew wears a watery grin, but he tries to blink back the emotions. He lifts a hand to trace down my jawline and his eyes follow his fingers. He swallows hard and forces his grin wider. He's trying to calm me down and put me in a better mood. Me, the raging bitchaholic. He's trying to make the best of a deadly situation, trying to hold it together and barely succeeding—for me. He's trying for me.

That hollow space inside me fills up with something I've never felt before. Like sunlight maybe. Or those little tickling wisps of dandelions that fly through the air.

I don't know what to do with this feeling. So, I revert to my old standby. Sarcasm. "Oh, I see how it is. I get shot so you can escape." I lean back and grin at him.

"Well, that would be the noble thing to do. Sacrifice yourself to save us poor men."

"Too bad I'm not noble then."

He laughs and tugs me closer. "I'm glad you're not." He plants a kiss on top of my head. And dammit all if that sweet gesture doesn't nearly break me. Because now, I really don't want to die. But as the Russians turn back to look at us, their mouths in straight, unsmiling lines, my chances of survival don't look good.

CHAPTER SEVEN

KATIE

W e stand on the path, watching the trees and waiting for what feels like an eternity. But we don't hear gunshots ring out.

Eventually, Alec says, "Well, no shots tells us one thing at least."

"What's that?" Kenneth asks, helping Alec reposition Sports Coat on his shoulder—the mob man hasn't shown any signs of waking.

"They're probably here to capture and not kill."

I slump against Danny and my knees get wobbly as momma's crap version of jello salad. I'm so relieved. And at the same time ... I feel this tiny ping. Of elation? Justification? Self-righteousness? I'm not sure. But after a minute, it gives me the strength to stand and move forward. I'm so, so relieved that I chose right. That we're not out here on a fool's errand while Heather and the guys are being ... I can't even finish the thought. Instead, I focus on what we're gonna do.

"If they're here for someone, it's gotta be Peter Brown." I push off Danny and move forward, taking the lead as the path turns from pavement into a worn dirt trail. "Let's go get us a gambling jerkwad." I walk into the forest, letting the canopy wipe out the moon and coat me in shadows. But I don't fucking shiver. Nope. I can't. Because I'm a woman on a mission. I'm a badass who's about to bring down one asshole and then take out another five. Yup. That's me.

In my mind, I start wearing leather and doing flips. All kinds of Cat Woman-y shit. And even though my tits grow like three cup sizes in my ima7ugination, they do not fucking hurt when I run.

I'm gonna rock this rescue mission.

That's what I tell myself all night long, as we walk through clouds of mosquitoes that wage a guerrilla war on us. They attack and retreat and attack and retreat. I even swallow one accidentally. It is not a fun night. We have no water, we're exhausted, and the guys have to take turns carrying our POW and guarding our rear. The one lucky thing about this island, is it seems that parrots and lizards are about the only animals. So we don't run into anything too scary as we wander through the dark.

It takes a long time, longer than I expect. And that means grumbling. It means complaining and cursing. But it also means random life stories come out. Of course, when Danny says he lost his virginity after he won a national championship at fourteen we all call out, "Lie!" He just grins and tells us he was actually fifteen. Kenneth ends up talking about the recipe book he's working on as dawn filters through the trees. He's about halfway through right now, but he's stuck on a dessert dish.

"It just feels like everything's been done." Kenneth explains as he shoulders Sports Coat.

"Man, I felt like that for awhile. Not for cooking. But I've been cliff diving, sky diving, all that shit all over the place. I was starting to feel like I was running out of things to do," Alec agrees.

"What broke you out of your rut?" Kenneth grunts, shifting his burden.

"Not what. Who." Alec's response is curt. But he steps forward to take the lead and his eyes land on mine. He holds my gaze for a second and his eyes burn holes through my skin, down to my very soul. Then he turns and goes tromping through the trees.

He takes my breath with him.

Not fair. I still want to be pissed. But that look, that look. That's a look I've only ever read about. That's a look I've never thought I'd see in real life. And Alec just gave it to me.

WE MAKE it to the waterfall by mid-afternoon. It's only supposed to be a half day walk to get up here, but the guys have had a huge fucking lump of human to carry. A couple times, I could have sworn our prisoner woke up, but then his eyes would roll back and he'd fall limp. Checking on him slowed us down. Plus, all our adrenaline wore off. After the crazy night with no sleep, I am so exhausted. I'm covered in sweat and mosquito bites. My hair has been tangled in so many branches that it looks like a tumbleweed. In other words, I look like anyone who has a job outside during the summer in Oklahoma. Pretty sure you couldn't pick me out of a line up of swamp monsters. I stick to the back of the group, in the hope that the guys will look at me a little bit less.

But how I look is nothing compared to Peter Brown.

We come upon him at the waterfall, as expected. The path curves and opens up into a bit of a clearing, where wide black stones make amazing little spots for the sunbathing billionaires who rent this island. The waterfall is a gorgeous, narrow trickle that spills down a steep series of black cliffs like a white ribbon. It splashes into a wading pool that's too perfectly kidney-shaped to be natural. The second I see all that water, I want nothing more than to jump into it. I want to drink it, bathe in it, and hide in it from the fucking bugs.

Kenneth's hand stops me as I step forward. He points through the trees and brush. There, in the middle of the water, is Peter Brown. Only, the man is so swollen and blotchy he does not look like himself anymore. He still has his buzzed brown hair and infant-sized ears—those are recognizable from behind. But his back is so covered in welts from mosquito bites that it looks misshapen. Parts of it are so red they're almost bleeding because he's clearly scratched them up. And though we've been in the shade, Peter Brown clearly got a sunburn yesterday because when he turns to face us, bits of skin are peeling off his nose. It looks like someone's taken a cheese grater to it. All in all, Peter Brown looks like something that the ER nurses would call "an interesting case." Heather and I used to hang out with this girl named Lisa who worked in the ER, and based on her stories, I never want to be an interesting case. I cross all my fingers and toes and pray that we do not end up looking the same. I mean, he is mirror-breakingly bad right now.

"Peter!" Alec yells. His voice is strong, commanding. The way my voice never sounds even when I practice 10,000 times. Heather tried once or twice to turn me into a phone sex operator. She thinks my laugh is cute and my innocent voice would appeal to guys. But I tossed that idea of hers in the trash where it belonged, right next to her suggestion that we ride across the country in a Greyhound bus and flash every car that drove by.

Peter Brown takes one looks at us and starts to run, I mean wade, because he is still submerged to his waist in the pool under the waterfall. Alec doesn't hesitate. He runs to the edge of the pool and leaps in, sending water everywhere as he chases down our target. Danny drops Sports Coat on the ground carelessly and Kenneth hands over the closet rod. Danny takes it with a nod of thanks. Then—again using some kind of guy-magic-mojo that's unspoken and total horseshit—they split up and go around opposite sides of the pool.

I stay back in case our prisoner wakes up or Peter tries to lunge past Alec. Well, really, I stay back because I have no idea what I'm doing. I don't know how to catch people. My daddy might have taken me shooting, but my hunting skills are Elmer Fudd level at best.

My guys have no such imposter syndrome issues. They slink around the pool like they're bounty hunters, calling out things like, "I'm at eight o'clock!"

I don't even know if Alec can hear them. Between Peter

Brown and Alec, the pool has been turned into a white, frothing pit of foam. They are splashing and making so many waves that I'm pretty certain if any fish lived in this pond, they've gone and died of a heart attack. The rocks in the pool must be slippery or something because watching Alec pursue Peter is like watching a horror movie chase scene at a banana factory. Honest to God, it is the most ridiculous thing I have ever seen. They try so hard to run, when they would be faster walking. But—men. In order to run, both of them have to lift their knees up super high out of the water, so they basically look like hopping, waddling, basilisk lizards—the kind that run across the water with their knees all splayed out. Only, these men aren't as talented as the lizards. They are slipping and sliding all over the place. And the the tension I can feel mounting in my chest—this need to apprehend Peter so that we can try to find out about these gangsters: who they are, what makes them tick, how to get them to release Heather and her guys —is at complete war with the epic ridiculousness of the chase in front of me.

Peter Brown pinwheels his arms every other step because he's sliding around so much. He's nearly to the edge of the pool on the opposite side when he notices Danny. Immediately, he changes direction. He changes again when he sees Kenneth, basically doing a full turn as his eyes flicker wildly around, looking for a place to escape. There isn't one. So, he dives.

Alec reaches into the water like he's a country boy gone noodling. He yanks Peter up by the hair, flips the former harem contender onto his back, and starts wading toward me, floating Peter across the top of the water like a bumpy, pink log.

Victory! Danny and Kenneth throw their arms in the air like they've done something. Well ... if it's a group celebration ... I join in and stick my arms up. Then I clap for Alec, who rolls his eyes but can't hold in a little grin.

I breathe a sigh of satisfaction. One helicopter down. One gangster down. One gambling motherfucker who brought the gangsters here down. My guys and I make a pretty good team. We could be superheroes—well, Alec could, anyway. He tosses Peter up onto the rocks and we surround the trembling man.

"I already told you, I can't go back!" Peter blubbers, as soon as he can get words out. All his smooth scheming appears to have sweated out of him in the sauna that is this forest. "They'll kill me."

"Yeah, we know about your gambling problem," I say.

"I'm not hurting anyone out here—"

I hold up a hand and cut Peter off. "That's where you're wrong. Your little loan shark buddies are here. With guns. For you."

"What!?" Peter's eye bulge.

I jerk my head toward Sports Coat, who's just starting to moan. His eyes still haven't opened.

Peter walks over and bends down, looking at the trussed-up gangster. He looks back over at me and shakes his head. "This guy isn't with the crew I borrowed cash from."

It feels like Peter just hit me in the stomach with Danny's curtain rod. The air rushes out of my lungs. "What?!"

CHAPTER EIGHT

HEATHER

They lock us up in the kitchen. On the hard-as-fuck, tiled floor. And they don't let us get dressed first. They are first-class, french-fry-for-dick assholes. Those Russian douchebags, with the help of Rubin and Reval, tie us all to the worktable legs.

"Scared I'll take your toy away again?" I spit at Suity as he ties me.

He doesn't answer. I don't know if it's because he doesn't understand my taunt or doesn't want to answer. He just moves on. And that dismissal makes me feel powerless, which just sparks my fire even more. I'm gonna break out of here, trap Suity, learn Russian, and then mock him until he's a sniveling puddle of snot on the floor. Just wait. And I'll give him a bowl haircut. *Bowl!* Fucker.

I can't even talk to the other guys at first, because stupid-ass Suity McGunpants keeps watch. We just stare at each other in silence. BJ's eyes flicker between me and the Russians constantly, like he's not sure who's scarier. Andrew stares at a spot in the floor and Jeremiah cranes his neck to look all around the kitchen—who the hell even knows why. I fume. I want to spit fire but these jerkwads can't even appreciate my insults.

Blob searches the fridge and pulls out leftovers. The Russians eat while we watch.

BJ is the first to ask, "Yo, could I get some of that?"

They turn to look at him.

He shrugs. "Hey, just an innocent bystander here. I didn't take your money. Shit. If I could, I'd sign that cash over to you, right now."

I glare at him.

"What?" He stares back, unapologetic. "I would. You should just sign a check and give 'em what they want so we can all go home."

I laugh. "You seriously think they're gonna let us go home?"

BJ's face gets stony and I roll my eyes. God, Katie should have done an IQ test when she screened these guys. Idiots. She gave me idiots. Her face pops into my head for a second, and I'm glad once more that she's not here. Only, for the first time, I wonder where the fuck she is. Is she seriously sleeping through all this? All day? I shake my head. If that's the case, if I find out later she's been sleeping—my default rage sputters. No. I can't be pissed at her. Not for sleeping, not for anything, really. Katie's my girl.

I wish I was a lesbian, not for the first time. If I was, she'd be it for me. Fuck this stupid addiction to dick. That's what started this whole she-bang. If I didn't want dick, we wouldn't have come here for harem tryouts. If we hadn't come here for harem tryouts, that story wouldn't have gotten in that online magazine. If that story hadn't been published, then—I hate Anthony Drake all over again. But there's a flaw in my logic. Rubin and Reval took a spot in my competition. They were supposed to get the money out of me. So, the Russians have known about me all along.

Dammit.

I glare at the twins, who are currently shoveling Kenneth's steak with balsamic reduction and feta cheese into their mouths; they look like four-year-olds trying to stuff every gummy bear in their trap before mom sees. And I'm jealous. Because that shit is good. I roll my eyes. "So, you're gonna starve the prisoners?"

Suity stares at me a moment as he gulps down a mouthful of food. He jerks a head toward Reval, who comes over and undoes my ties.

At first, I think that means they're going to let me eat, but Reval gestures for me to sit in the seat farthest from the food. J2 follows up that invitation with a wave of his gun, so I sit.

Reval looks at me. And I can see the wheels turning in his head. And some kind of revelation-type thing goes on as he eyes me. Immediately, my hackles rise. I want to live, but this look he's giving me is weird. It's like the look that women get when they come into the salon and they're about to change their whole fucking hairstyle—the locks I've worked on for six months, highlighting and feathering them to perfection, are suddenly gonna go *poof*—that look in their eyes means they're about to request a goddamn pixie cut when they have the squarest jaw in the world. Because they've got an itch. An itch that's leading them to commit hair suicide. Reval has hair suicide face.

I start to shake my head before he even opens his mouth. I hold up a finger. "No, not gonna do it."

"I did not say —"

"Not gonna do it. Whatever it is, it's not happening."

Unfortunately the twins exchange a look, and I swear to God, those motherfuckers have ESP. Rubin glances over at me with a little bit of hope in in his eyes

"Heather. We could maybe help you." He holds out his hand.

As if I'm gonna touch him after everything that's happened. I raise a brow—but not, like, just raise a brow. I mean *raise a brow*—Jerry Springer, no-you-didn't style. What the fuck to they think? Do they think I'm stupid? Do they think I'm actually gonna trust them after I found out that they are somehow connected to the assholes with guns? Speaking of this connection ...

I turned to Suity McGunpants. "How do you know the double mint twins?"

"Double mint?"

I wave off his confusion. I point. "How do you know Rubin and Reval?"

Rubin nods toward Suity and says, "He works for father. All of them do."

I stiffen. Father? I specifically asked every guy in this

competition about their family. I did not want drama. The twins said they didn't have a father. That confession of theirs led to goddamn sympathy sex. Sympathy sex—meaning I went all out for the double facial when I *hate* facials. Oh, I am about to pitch a fit. Those motherfuckers. They are double disqualified. They lied to me so they could get sympathy sex. Then they bring assholes with guns to my island.

"So, your dad set up this lotto buying scam with Blob—"

"Boris, was to be the buyer, yes." Rubin clasps his hands. "When things went poorly ... my father sent us to find you."

Blob butts in. "They were to get monies back."

"But you failed, so he sent guys to shoot me dead?" I shake my head.

Both twins wince. "Our father is very one-minded when it comes to money. This project was very large."

J2 interrupts. "Yes, there was much face riding on it."

"But, if you marry one of us then the money is ours by marriage, no?" Rubin tries to sound reasonable. Like he's making some rational proposal. Some business deal.

I laugh. I fucking laugh so hard my tits hurt from shaking and I have to put an arm around them to stop it.

Suity's nostrils flare. He's offended by the fact that I turned down the twins proposal. "Their offer is most generous. More than we would give. You sign wedding papers. The money their family's. Maxim pays back what is owed for money people."

Andrew pipes up from his spot on the floor, "He has investors?"

Suity nods. "Yes, these. People who share the monies. Get more back."

"People invested in the lottery?" I'm skeptical. "That ain't a thing."

Andrew chimes, "Actually, there have been articles citing mathematicians doing it. They wait until the pot is big enough, calculate the total amount needed to buy every ticket available, get investors and tell them they'll get a guaranteed payout at a certain percentage—"

BJ whistles. "Well, fuck me sideways. Sign me up for that shit."

Andrew cocks his head and studies me. "Most places have made it illegal now."

I roll my eyes, "But of course—backwoods Oklahoma is behind the times." I sigh.

"It only works if you get every ticket." Andrew shrugs.

I run my hand down my face. "And of course, my one singular ticket—"

Blob interjects. "You cause many problems." His hand smacks down on the table hard enough to make their plates jump with a clank.

Rubin holds up a hand to stop him. "But, fate is good, is it not? Without this issue, we would not have met Heather. She is the one."

Oh, no I am fucking not. But I smile, because what the fuck else am I gonna do right now.

Reval stands from his chair and wipes his hands on a napkin, before walking over to me. Unlike the rest of us, who are still naked, the twins have at least wrapped pool towels around their waists. "Heather. Beautiful, Heather. Marry us. Either one, no hard feelings."

"Yes hard feelings," Blob interjects with a snicker. "Dick is hard feelings, yes? Marriage has many hard feelings."

No one but him laughs at his lame joke.

I put a hand on my hip and stare from twin to twin. They actually think this is possible. Do they have that kind of pull with their father? Ugh... I'm not sure why I'm even listening to them. They're idiots. "I don't see the benefit in this marriage thing for me. You're basically forcing me into an even worse marriage than the one I just had, and then taking all my money." I push it back on them.

BJ speaks up for the first time in a long time. "Don't be a selfish bitch. Ever occur to you that if you do this—maybe they'll let us live?"

I narrow my eyes at him. Backstabbing Brooklyn fucker. Cares more about living than the fact I'd be selling myself into virtual slavery. But he has a point. It might be the only way any of us get out of this alive. I'm kind of annoyed by that. "I have to think about it."

"This is good deal, no?" Suity turns to BJ.

"Great deal. But, women," BJ shrugs like I'm being unreasonable.

The twins nod.

I almost walk over to J2 and tell him to shoot me now. I'm done with these sexist ding-dongs.

But Andrew calls me over. I walk away from the table, swiping some water bottles as I do. I toss a water bottle to Jeremiah and crack one open for Andrew and I to share.

"Hey!" BJ protests.

I just flip him off.

Behind me, Blob tells the others he's going back to the helicopter to check on Sasha. I don't know who the hell Sasha is, I'm just fucking glad to have one less crazy ass gunmen here with us. I do a quick head count. My team versus the baddies. It's Rubin, Reval, J2, and Suity Mcgunpants versus me, Andrew, BJ, and Jeremy. I've been untied. I reach down and loosen Andrew's ropes subversively as I try and weigh the odds of what might happen if we straight up fought. The twins have muscle but they don't know how to use it. But the guns ... now I motherfucking wish I had done what Andrew had said. I wish I had taken that gun. Then I wouldn't be here hemming and hawing. I'd go Annie Oakley on their ass.

Andrew says in a low voice, "Heather you should really think about this marriage offer. I wouldn't be so quick to dismiss the twins. Right now, they still want you. That's a bargaining chip."

I cross my arms under my breasts and that momentarily distracts him, as usual. I know Andrew's right. But it chuffs me to think I might have to stoop to that. I don't ever want to be married again. That was part of the point of this whole trip. But I don't really want to see these three poor guys (or Katie and her guys) get shot down either. I close my eyes and pray for the strength to be a martyr.

Then I put my fingers to my lips and whistle. Every head turns toward me. "I need some time to think about the damn marriage thing. But I'm not getting married without a goddamn dress or flowers. And my hair and makeup sure as hell aren't gonna look like this."

It takes a minute, because those twins really are goddamn slow. But when they understand what I said, both of them wear shit-eating grins. They think they've won. The superior-ass dicks.

I turn away from them. I turn away from Andrew and my guys, too. Because I don't know how long I can fake being reasonable. That's just not in my nature. The only reason I said those words at all was to give myself time to come up with a fucking plan. Because I am gonna stick it to those sons of bitches if it's the last thing I do.

CHAPTER NINE

KATIE

"Y ou're lying!" I scream at Peter Brown. He knows the guy on the ground. He has to!

Peter cringes away from me. "The guys I owe are from Jersey! The Warlock's Motorcycle Club."

I roar and then shove that slimy little shit. Even though he's twice my size, he stumbles back. "Don't mock me! Don't make fun of me right now!" I rage. "I can't deal with it."

"I'm not! Geez! Really, I'm not."

"You expect me to believe there's some fucking wizard gang?"

"That's their name! Shit!" Peter rubs his chest where I shoved him and then starts scratching at the bites there.

"Stop that, you'll make it worse," Kenneth tells him. "You don't want to open up any more of those bites."

How is he able to be reasonable right now? I almost want to shove him for it. I'm so pissed I don't even think I have color vision right now. Everything is black and white. And Peter's a black-hearted smear who needs to be erased.

"Die here or die there," Peter Brown mumbles. "Here's better than there. You don't know what they'd do."

"Why, would they cast a spell on you?" Danny mocks.

If I wasn't so freaked out, I'd high five him. Wizard fucking gang. Bullshit. The financial dark net dude I messaged didn't give me a name for whoever Peter Brown owed... dammit all. But Jersey sounds more likely than Russians.

"How big are the Warlocks?" Alec asks. "How many people?"

"Shit. I dunno. They're in a couple states."

"How many people in the gang you borrowed from?"

"I've seen maybe twenty."

Alec nods and puts his hands into his sopping suit pockets, thinking.

I don't know why he's wasting time asking questions about the Warlocks. It's not like they matter. They aren't the ones here. Dammit! I pace, rubbing my palms together. I'm not sure what to say or think or do. Did we just waste over it half a day coming up here for no reason? If these guys with guns have nothing to do with Peter Brown, then why the hell are they here?

I march over to Sports Coat and start kicking him. Not hard enough to seriously hurt him, but hard enough to get him to wake the fuck up.

"Katie—" Kenneth reaches for me, but I shrug him off and keep kicking.

"Don't," I growl. And for once my voice doesn't go all thin and reedy and uncertain. It's as dark and dangerous as I feel.

Sports Coat grunts and groans, and finally comes to. His pale eyes blink up at me and he stares around us, dazed. He probably has no idea where the hell he is. One second he was on the ground by his chopper, now he's by some forest pool. But I could care less about how he feels right now. My empathy is gone. I am only composed of a burning need-to-know in this moment.

"Who are you?"

He doesn't answer; he simply groans. When he realizes he can't move his arms, his jaw drops and he lifts his head to look down at his body. I take a second to admire our twine handiwork as it freaks him out. Then I get back to questioning. "Why did you come to this island? Who are you looking for?"

He opens his mouth to speak, but his throat is so dry that all that comes out is a half-hacking wheeze.

The guys have to help him up and lead him over to the water so he can get a drink. He sips the at the edge of the pool, using his tongue to lap since he can't use his hands. My guys join him and cup the water in their hands, wiping down their faces and refreshing themselves after our hike. We are all exhausted and tired, operating on no sleep, a massive crash after the adrenaline burst last night; we're also wallowing in disappointment. My throat aches too, but I'm too frazzled to stop and drink with them. I can't just kneel down next to Sports Coat and drink water, like 'no big deal.'

I'm amped. I'm freaking out. I chew a hole in my lip as I pace. I chose wrong. I chose wrong. Who knows what's happening to Heather right now because of this choice? My choice! I'm so fucking relieved that at least we followed Alec's advice and disabled the helicopter. Otherwise, these guys with guns could've flown her away. To who knows where. Because if these guys aren't here for Peter, who the hell else on the island has a skeleton in their closet?

After another tense minute, Alec jerks Sports Coat's face away from the water. I crouch down low so that I can look this asshole in the eyes. "Who sent you? Who are you here for?"

"No English," Sports Coat gasps.

I lean back inch and share a scared look with the guys. "No English. What the hell does that mean?"

But, even as I ask the question aloud, an eerie feeling creeps into my chest. There are only two guys on this island that are not native English speakers. And the very first time they got off Alec's plane I wondered what the hell was going on. But instead of injecting my normal Katie paranoia, I let it go. I was busy, so I let it go. They were never supposed to be eleven guys on this island, but I didn't follow up about it. I let those Russian twins waltz right into Heather's harem just because they were twins. And now whatever these crazy people are planning, it's all my fault.

CHAPTER TEN

HEATHER

I snuggle with Andrew on the floor of the kitchen when the sun rises. The asshole Russians don't give us clothes or food or jackshit. Apparently, humane treatment isn't a concept they care about. I fall asleep on him to thoughts of castration, to visions of lining my salon mirror with their shrunken little balls, shaved and painted red and green like Christmas ornaments.

When I wake up, the afternoon sun is beating down through the windows. I stare around the kitchen, blinking, wondering for a second if I just had a super drunken orgy with my harem candidates and dreamt the men-with-guns thing. I'm disoriented and not quite sure what's going on.

"Hey gorgeous," I hear in Andrew's voice coming from the other side of the kitchen. "Good afternoon. Sleep well?"

I rub my eyes and sit up. Everything comes flooding back to me. My eyes scan the kitchen, but I don't see any of the gangster jerkoffs. Andrew, BJ, and Jeremiah sit at stools around one of the three worktables in the room. They're speaking in low voices, passing each other dill pickles, chugging water, and eating huge chicken sandwiches. They're all still naked, but completely comfortable with it after all the time we've spent nude together. Andrew swats a fly away from their food. And everything looks normal, hunkydory, which is weird as fuck.

"What the hell?" I sit up and realize someone put a towel underneath my head while I slept. That was somewhat thoughtful. I give Andrew credit. No way I'm giving it to the twins. That towel is probably the only reason my head doesn't feel like it's about to pop off my neck. The rest of my body is sore as hell, though. When I stand, I realize that I've got red marks down my thighs from the grout lines in the tile.

"Hurry and eat before they get back," Andrew tells me.

"They're real? The Russians? Not a dream? What's going on?" I ask a million questions, my mouth shooting off everything that's running through my brain as I stretch my aching back. Fuck this thirties shit. I used to spend a ton of nights sleeping on floors in my twenties. And none of those made me feel like death. Of course, none of those involved guntoting Russian mafia men either.

BJ moans into his sandwich as he watches my boobs while I stretch. He swallows and says, "I wish we had enough time to fuck before they get back. I hate that we got interrupted yesterday. Blue balls all night, man."

I shoot him a dirty look. I hate that we got interrupted, too. But, priorities. I open my mouth to tell him off as I walk over to their table, but Andrew starts to explain what's been happening. I decide an explanation of what the hell's going on is more important than reaming BJ's ass. I sit down on a free stool and grab the bag of bread. I take a slice and eat it plain. My stomach doesn't seem ready for more.

Andrew says, "The guy with the big nose came back last night—"

"Blob," I supply. "I nicknamed him Blob."

Jeremiah looks at me and raises his brow. "Why the hell'd you do that?"

I wave him off. "It's not important. It's just easier to keep track of people. Blob's the one with the gut. J2 is the Arnold look-a-like. Suity McGunpants—self-explanatory. Just so we're all on the same page."

The guys exchange an amused smirk. BJ asks with a full mouth, "So, what's your nickname for me?"

"Little Foot. Because you know small feet, small ..." I smirk at his scowl as I take another bite of bread and place my feet in Andrew's lap. Both Andrew and Jeremiah choke down their laughter, trying to hide it with their sandwiches and their hands.

"You're a goddamn bitch!" BJ goes all Brooklyn on me, glaring down his crooked nose.

I shrug. "An honest bitch, though. Not a back-stabbing, turncoat, traitor bitch like you."

"Excuse me for not wanting to die!"

"Coward!"

"Crazy!"

"If you survive this, you're totally gonna be a cuck," I tell him. "I'm buying a cage for your tiny penis. And then I'm gonna fuck guys in front of you and your dick is gonna swell and that cage is gonna hurt like fuck, but I'm not gonna let you come."

He goes all squinty eyed. "What the fuck? If I survive this, there's no way in hell I want to be part of your harem. You got some goddamned Russian gangsters breathing down your neck. You're a dead woman."

"Whoa! Whoa, whoa!" Andrew interjects, but not before I grab his water bottle and chuck it at BJ's fat head.

"Bitch, I'll cut you!"

"Please, try," I sneer.

BJ stands up and I can see his little dick is standing at attention.

I jerk my chin at it. "You like the idea of being my cuck, don't you, fucker?"

"No! Shut up." BJ sits back down, covering his dick. It's so small his hand completely covers it.

"Just remember that next time you try to backstab me, asshole." I seethe.

Andrew strokes my arm and helps me sit back down. "Heather. We have a plan. Calm down. We're gonna get out of here. Okay? Just calm down and listen to the plan." He gathers up my feet and puts them back onto his lap.

"Before the plan, I just ... what the hell's *my* nickname?" Jeremiah blurts out.

I can see the curiosity burning in his eyes. I roll my own. I point at Jeremiah. "You're Thumper. Cause of your last name. Bible thumper." I wink at him. "And because you're good at thumping."

His chest puffs up a bit as I turn to Andrew. "You're just Doctor. Cause that's hot all on its own."

I bat my eyes at Andrew and say sweetly, "You were saying something about Blob and getting out of here?"

Andrew snorts at all my names before he answers. "Blob came in last night and said that the helicopter wouldn't start. He said he couldn't find Sasha. And that the chopper radio wasn't working. They all ran out. I loosened my ropes the rest of the way and untied these two shortly after."

"So they've been gone for hours?" I stare at each and every one of the guys in shock and horror. "What the hell are we still doing here!? Why the hell didn't you wake me up?"

"We tried."

BJ snorts. "An airhorn wouldn't wake you up when you're out, Heather."

I flip him off and stare at Andrew, running my hands through my hair. Ugh, it's a complete disaster. "Why haven't we run?"

"They've been searching the villas for Sasha all night and all morning. We expect they'll be back soon," Andrew says before taking a bite of his pickle.

"But—" I stare at the three of them and they shake their heads. How can they act like this is Sunday brunch at grandma's? Why aren't we running for our motherfucking lives? And wait ... if the gangsters been searching the villas, why haven't they found Katie? Or any of the staff?

"Where's everyone else?"

Jeremiah's face darkens and he's the one who answers. "Heard something about a boat speeding away. Looks like the staff left us behind."

Ohhh ... that makes my blood boil. Those selfish fucks. Are they even gonna report us to the authorities? Are there even any authorities who'd come? Did they take Katie? God, I hope they took Katie. First off, I hope she's fucking safe. Secondly, that bitch knows I'll pay for a private army to come in here and wipe these guys out.

I cross my fingers and motherfucking hope that Katie was on that boat and that she's gonna send some hot GI Joes my way. I promise to pay them back in cash and sexual favors for life.

"What are you doing?" BJ asks.

I look down at my fingers and say, "Just hoping those assholes who forgot about us when they hopped in a boat didn't really forget about us."

Jeremiah says, "I don't think we should count on that."

"You gotta steal my only hope? That's kind of a prick move, Thumper. That's a strike-against-you kinda move."

He rolls his eyes. "You think the harem bullshit is still on with all this? Get your head in the game. It's life and death right now."

Out. He's totally out. And BJ was out but that cuck thing was kinda hot ... he's hanging on by a thread. Maybe. I glare at Andrew, daring him to disappoint me, too. If he's gonna do it, he better do it now. Just rip off the band aid and get it the fuck over with. Andrew just sets down his pickle and starts massaging my feet.

I gulp. Damn he's so sweet. He gives me a soft smile and lets me know that idiot Jeremiah's just a fool. At least, that's what I interpret his smile to mean.

Andrew gestures toward Jeremiah, who sets down his sandwich, wipes his mouth, and gives a nasty little smile, the kind men give after they've fucked your ass too hard. It's self-satisfied and pricky. "Well now, based on what we've overheard, and the recon I did after Andrew untied me, it seems our little friends are just as stranded here we are."

"What?"

"Their helicopter isn't working. Guess maybe the staff disabled it before they took off. Their cell phones don't work. Neither do ours, by the way, tried that. But it looks like they're stuck." His eyes have this weird gleam. I'm starting to think he might be a little cray-cray.

"So?" I still have no clue why we haven't run into the forest. Why we aren't hiding in the thick-ass trees? "They still have guns! Did y'all forget about that?"

And this is where Jeremiah's face turns scary. He gets an aggressive, maniacal look that I have never in my life seen before. "Oh, we remember. Do you remember how I told you my parents were a bit odd?"

I nod, even though my memories of chatting with Jeremiah are hazy. Too many men—they all blur together a bit.

I'm not sure if Jeremiah sees through my response or he's just getting into being all dramatic. He starts waving his hands like a preacher and I decide he's Mr. Drama. "My dad's a prepper. Thinks the world's gonna end and thinks he's gonna *want* to survive the apocalypse. Made me run drills my whole life." He leans back in his seat, seeming to forget he's on a stool. He loses his balance a bit and has to grab the table so he doesn't tunk right over onto the floor.

I swallow. Great. His dad sounds about as sharp as a marble —that's one of Katie's favorite sayings. Jeremiah's face doesn't make me feel too confident that the son's not as nuts as the father. He can't even sit on a stool.

Jeremiah keeps talking, explaining why the fuck we're stuck with prisoner status when he knows how to build tree forts and hunt shit. I'd rather be playing fucking Tarzan and Jane right now than sitting here.

Jeremiah gets his hands going again. "You can run from tyrants. But they'll chase you. We're all stuck sharing this island. Without that chopper, they've got no way to leave. And they've got the weapons. How do you think that's gonna work out?"

Tyrants? Really? He had to go there. I sigh but I shut my trap. Because for some reason, Andrew's on board with this.

Jeremiah lifts his eyebrows like he's clever. "We want to lure them into thinking they've got the upper hand. That's why, when they do come back, we're gonna all act like we're tied up and miserable."

My stomach drops in disappointment. I cover my face with my hands. This sounds like the worst fucking plan ever. "And this is gonna help us, how?"

"It's gonna give us the time we need to build a bomb."

CHAPTER ELEVEN

KATIE

I'm about to break down. Tears shine in my eyes and I chew my lip as I realize we're half a day away from getting back to Heather. Anything could happen in that half a day. Anything could've already happened. We came all the way up here ... for nothing.

Alec strides over to me. I can't look up and meet his eyes. I can't bear to see his disappointment in me. I can't bear to have him critique me like my mother would. Or even just give me a pitying look—a look that means he thinks Heather's gone. I fucked up so big.

Instead of talking, Alec gently takes the gun out of my hands. He takes the gun out of his waistband. And he hands them both to Kenneth.

Alec's arms wrap around me. I'm picked up and cradled against his chest. I think he's about to give me a hug, a hug I don't deserve. My arms reach for him—but suddenly, my body goes sailing through the air.

Smack!

I hit the water in the pond and sink down hard. The floor of the pool comes at me like boards come at a hockey player—too fast. My ass gets bruised as a peach on the stones beneath the surface. Fuck! This pool is so shallow; it's like a goddamn kiddie pool at the base of this waterfall. Only, it's lined in stone and not plastic. Motherfucking ouch! I push myself up to the surface and sputter as I stand, coughing up water. My dress is drenched. But it's not heavy. There's not enough of it to be heavy. The water rolls off this sheer material and slides down my thighs.

There's a huge splash behind me. I turn to see Alec has jumped into the pool.

My heart is racing in my ribs from having flown through the air. My ass is throbbing, pain radiates up my lower back. My mind is stuck somewhere between furious and shocked. The two emotions pull me in opposite directions until I feel stretched as tight as a botoxed brow.

Alec strides toward me, his look dark and intent. He smiles and his teeth gleam in the light, like a fucking shark. Fury and shock fade. Instead, I feel hunted.

"What was that?" I ask, backing away as I wring out my hair. I try not to let my voice tremble. But shit, he looks mad at me. Is he pissed about everything?

"That was getting you out of your own head, Katie," he responds. "I could see you chastising yourself, blaming yourself. You can't do that."

What? His words blindside me. That is not what I was expecting to hear. Anger—sure. But a lecture? Who the hell is he to tell me to drop my guilt?

As typical of me, I lie. I hate the way he's looking at me. I hate him pointing out my flaws even though I deserve it. I hate that he's making everything uncomfortable. "I don't feel guilty."

"Lie!" Danny calls out across the water.

I flip him the bird.

"Well, who cares if I do? So what? My best friend's down there. You think I'm supposed to feel good about this fuck up?" I cross my arms defensively, which just gets my wet dress tangled and makes it edge up my thighs. I'm not sure my ass is completely covered anymore, but my guys have all moved to the other side of the pool, guarding Peter Brown and Sports Coat, so I don't really worry about it.

Alec shakes his head. "No. I don't expect you to feel good about it. But stop blaming yourself for it. Because we all agreed to come out here. We can't predict the future. We didn't know Peter'd turn out to be a useless dead end."

"Hey!" Peter starts to protest, but Kenneth just smacks him on the side of the head.

Alec continues, "Nobody's right all the time, Katie. You need to give yourself a break."

"I can't. What if—"

Alec steps closer, casting a shadow over me as he glares down at me. He's a dark, unrelenting wall of muscle and I'm intimidated as fuck. But I'm also turned on. "You can and you will. Because I'm gonna make you." With that last line Alec strides towards me like a panther. He's tall, dark, and dangerous. Instinct makes me take a step back.

"That's not nice," I whisper.

Alec cracks a half smile. "What about me ever made you think I was a nice guy? When I left you panting on the plane? When I dared you in order to force you to go on a date with me? When I cock-blocked those other two? When I fucked you in front of them?"

Shit. My pussy is molten. I swallow hard and back further away. "I get what you're trying to do. You're trying to distract me. And you're doing a really good job. But Heather could be dead right now and I don't have time for games."

"This isn't a game. This is reality. You can't let your mind get stuck in a cycle of 'what if' or 'if I had only.' It's unhealthy. You think I don't have regrets? I've lost people. Lots of people. But if you sink into that thought process, it's like quicksand. That shit will pull you under. You can't breathe down there. Trust me. I know." His voice gets gravelly with emotion.

Pity, sympathy, and empathy are car crushers ... and my heart's an old Buick. They smash me flat. I stop backing up. My fear is overcome. Because Alec has seen shit. Lived through it. I know he has. I can see it in his dark look. "I'm sorry for your loss."

He doesn't respond. He just reaches out for me and grabs me around the waist again. I let him. This time, he does give me the hug I originally anticipated. He crushes my body to his. He pulls me up high so that my toes float in the water. My skirt rides even further up my ass as his hands clench my waist.

He speaks into my hair. "I can't watch you fall down that rabbit hole. It can take years to climb out."

My throat constricts. My chest tightens. "I don't know how to avoid it." It's the truth.

"We focus on the future. Plan for the future. We plan for contingencies. We plan for every single thing you want to do when we get back down there. You want to shoot them up? Fine. We plan that. But you hold onto the future. That plan. You gotta fill your mind up with so many plans that there isn't any room left for 'what ifs' or 'if I'd only' ..."

Plans. Plans. "I can try that."

Alec squeezes me even harder, his hands slipping from my waist down to my ass. He pulls my legs to wrap around him, getting me as close as possible. "Good." His buries his face in my neck, so his answer is muffled, but his tone is thick with emotion.

Suddenly his hands flex and his fingers dig into my ass. He pulls the cheeks apart. Then his finger slides down my crack and hits my slit. Since I have no panties, he can immediately feel just how wet his 'asshole persona' has made me. "Mmmm," he moans. His finger circles my opening, then traces softly up and down my lips.

"Fucking turn around, now!" I see Danny push Peter Brown, forcing the other man to look away from where Alec's raised my dress. Kenneth stands, after having rolled Sports Coat in the other direction. After they've ensured the others aren't looking, both my guys stare solemnly at me as Alec continues to tease my opening.

My thoughts start to float like feathers. Wispy, fluttering.

Until his finger plunges into me and every thought I have is blown away. "No," I moan. But I don't mean it.

"No? You want me to stop?" Alec asks, bending his finger so he can gently tap my g-spot.

"No." The word just slips out.

"Okay," he sighs and starts to withdraw his finger.

I panic when I realize what he's doing. "No, I mean, we shouldn't be doing this, but no ... don't stop."

Alec's grin is feral. "If you want me to keep going, I'm gonna finger you in front of them. Kenneth and Danny are gonna get to watch you writhe and moan and ride my finger like it's a little cock."

He doesn't play fair. Because as he describes all that, his hand digs into my ass and pulls me back so that the hand inside my pussy can grind against my clit as his finger fucks me.

I can't even respond because my mind is reduced to flashes of color and electric sensations. There's a fucking '90s rave going on inside my body and the light is dancing. But then it stops. Alec slides his finger out of me and flips me around so my back is to him. "Put your hands around my neck," he growls into my ear.

I link my hands around him and he slides my dress up, exposing my pussy to the view of Danny and Kenneth. Danny checks to make sure Peter's still looking away. Once, he's reassured himself, this is a private show, he starts to stroke himself over his shorts.

Alec wraps my legs backward around his waist, so that I

arch forward a little and my pussy is exposed, pointed right at them. I feel a moment of embarrassment before Alec plunges two fingers inside me and scissors them. His other hand slides across my chest just enough for him to grab my nipple through my dress in a vice grip. He tweaks my nipple and sensation shoots down to my womb.

"You're a naughty little girl. Letting them watch you like this in the open. Are you my bad girl, Katie?" Alec whispers right into my ear before biting my neck.

Shit! Embarrassment is forgotten as lust makes me buck like a bronco. All the hormones and emotions and fear and anxiety that have been pooling in my system burn up as I turn into an inferno of lust. Nothing else can survive this heat.

He tugs again on my nipple and bends his head forward to nip at my neck. I feel his cock swelling against my ass, nudging against my crack.

"Open those eyes and look at your men while they stare at you," Alec orders.

I do. Danny's halfway to his own orgasm, by the look of things. And Kenneth has a dark, hungry look in his eyes. I dig my legs into Alec's back and lift my pelvis more, trying to give them an even better view.

Alec's palm smacks my clit as his fingers work me. That earns a moan. So he repeats it. *Smack. Smack.* The fifth one sends me over the edge. "Fuck!" I dig my hands into the back of his neck, scratching him as he makes me come.

He keeps working me though. He doesn't stop. He just pulls his fingers out from inside me and uses those wet digits to circle my clit, soaking it with my juices. Once it's slippery to the touch, he pinches it gently between his fingers and then pulls. I blow like a transformer. The orgasm is so intense, it's literally a flash of light behind my eyes before everything goes dark. My toes curl and my muscles spasm and my body short circuits before going limp. My mind is one hundred percent wiped.

Alec finally stops when my arms drop from around his neck. He pulls me flush against him, circling my ribcage and my hips, and holding me as I come back down. "God, I want to fuck you right now," he whispers.

I blink. "What?" My eyes and ears are still not functioning at full capacity.

His fingers knead my flesh. Then he takes one hand and traces up the curve of my hip. He reaches up and tugs my skirt back down, saying, "I love this fucking dress. Hiking up here behind you, watching the bottom of your ass cheeks peek out from the skirt—best view I've ever had. Made hauling that useless fucker up here worth it."

I giggle. "You're crazy."

"Question is, are you crazy enough to fuck me here in this pool?" Alec nuzzles my hair as he asks the question.

My heart pumps faster. Heat gathers at my center. "After what you just did, it's not that much more. Is that what you want?" I ask. But as my mind reboots, thoughts of Heather and her guys come back online. The sick guilty feeling doesn't return. But the sense of urgency, the need to get to them, to help if we can, does.

Alec leans to the side to look at me. And it's as if he can read my thoughts. "Not yet."

I give him a little shrug. "Sorry."

"No sorry allowed." He flips me back around to face him. I straddle his hips as he pulls my skirt back down over my ass.

On the shore, Danny calls out, "Boo!" as he senses the end of the show.

Alec ignores him, dragging his hand up my side until he can cup my chin. He places a chaste kiss on my lips. He pulls back and rests his forehead against mine. For a minute, we just breathe each other in. Then he asks, "Head clear? Are you ready to hike back down and make a plan for what we're gonna do when we get there?"

I nod.

"Good." He smacks my ass and drops me in the water. I'm not expecting it and fall backward, my face slipping under the surface of the shallow pool.

"Dick wad!" I call out after I surface, spluttering again. Alec is already wading back to shore on his own.

He turns back over his shoulder and grins. "That's what you get for mixing me up with a nice guy!"

I flip him off. But the inside of my chest blooms like one of those time-lapse roses. Dammit all. Alec might not want to be called a nice guy. But I know better.

CHAPTER TWELVE

Apparently, essence of lime is flammable. I have to ask what the fuck essence is.

It's really fucking annoying to have gap-toothed, loony prepper Jeremiah sneer at me and say, "The peel, grated," like I'm some uncouth, backwoods idiot. Excuse me, I'm not the one who grew up digging holes to poop in, thank you.

For some reason—that I don't ask about after the stupid lime essence Q&A—lime plus a pressure cooker or two, plus whatever the hell else ... equals explosion.

Jeremiah's been bustling around the kitchen grabbing and sawing things apart. He's pulled apart Kenneth's recipe printer and extracted a 'laser diode' or something. He shoved that into a flashlight. And he's got a whole pile of crap next to him on the floor at the back of the kitchen and he's looking happy as a pig in slop.

Andrew's busy measuring out and mixing different amounts of bleach and rubbing alcohol and then dipping rags in his little mix. We each get one to hide under our ass because, apparently, that combo makes chloroform. The better to knock the Ruskies out with ... if it comes to that.

Next to him is a container of oven cleaner. He's cut off and peeled back the lid. We're apparently gonna take that and a bottle of bleach with us on the run, because homemade fucking mustard gas is a solid backup plan.

BJ is over at his table, using a knife sharpener to sand down the edges of pie pans. Because he "rocks the disc golf, yo"—his words, which somehow justify him turning pie pans into Xena-like death chakras. Because Xena powers are a real thing.

All this shit makes my teeth clench. But it's better than feeling powerless. Even if we fuck ourselves up, it's better than handing everything over to the damn Russians. If Katie made it out of here alive and I don't ... at least I took care of all that lawyer shit right away and she'll get my money. But she'd better not give a goddamned cent to her black-mouthed mother. Fuck. I shoulda' put that in the require-ments. *If I make it off this island, it's getting added,* I think, as I grab another lime.

We're all working in our respective "tied up" spaces, so that when the Russians get back, we can just throw our stuff on the shelves under the worktables and act all forlorn. But I got stuck grating limes for the bomb. As if I'm the dunce of this group. Grating limes is like cutting men's hair—boring and simple as fuck. It's all tiny little trims that are dull. After an hour, I start grating in a spiral pattern just for something to do.

"How much a' this shit do you need?" I ask for the twentieth time. Ugh. I never went on road trips, so I never got the chance to experience the dullness that is miles and miles of flat land punctuated by occasional roadkill. My parents were always too strung out for that shit. But still. This sitting in the same spot and doing the same thing is about to drive me bananas. Can't I do something bigger? More important than damn limes?

"Why don't we play a game?" Andrew suggests.

"Anything!" I respond. "I'm dying."

"Never have I ever—" BJ suggests.

I laugh. "Dunno that you'll find much I haven't tried."

Jeremiah even grins from whatever electrical crap he's working on. "I mightta' won that game before we got here, but now, shit, orgies, food sex, getting kidnapped by gunmen—"

"One round," BJ insists. "Let's just see if I can stump you."

I finish grating one lime and grab another as I say, "Give it your best shot."

BJ thinks awhile. "Never have I ever swam with sharks."

All of us stop what we're doing and look up. "Dammit!"

BJ laughs and slaps his knee. "Yes!"

I point my grater at him. "Just so you know, I'm pretty sure Katie had something like that lined up for us."

BJ shudders. "No way. Out. Sharks are a no go."

"I didn't know they had a lot of sharks near here," Jeremiah says.

"It's the ocean—" My sentence is interrupted by footsteps on the path outside.

We all freeze for a second in panic. Andrew's the first to recover. "Shit. Quick, hide everything and tie yourself up!"

We all start shoving bowls and crap under the tables. Luckily, that Kenneth guy used every spare inch of storage space. So I don't think the mobsters will notice that we've moved things around. I toss my tools under the table I share with Andrew. I start to shove my limes under there. All the guys are already re-tying their hands—they didn't have to put away twenty damn limes. Fuck! My hands shake with nerves and the new lime I'd just started to grate rolls away from me. I shove the rest of the limes into the bag and under the table. Then I scramble on my knees toward that green motherfucker.

The door starts to open.

Shit! I ditch the lime and crawl back to my spot, boobs banging my damn arms every few seconds. I tie myself up next to Andrew with shaking hands and sit my ass down on my chloroform rag to hide it. I'm still pulling the rope tight with my teeth when the Russians walk in.

"You won't get out so easy," Suity McGunpants mocks me.

I drop my mouth from the rope and glare at him. Little does he know. Idiot. Fuck. I have to fight a smirk. I suck at being all passive and shit. But I gotta try. Channel Katie, I tell myself. Channel the fuck out of Katie.

Rubin picks up the lime I dropped. "What is this?" He rolls it over, examining it. Luckily, I'd just started zesting, so there's only a small chunk where the peel is worn down to the white pith.

Crap!

My eyes dart to Jeremiah, and his eyes widen in a "do something" glare. Fuck him! Fuck! What do I do?

"I was hungry," Andrew says. "We've been here all fucking day. I got desperate."

Oh, thank goodness. Andrew to the rescue. Shit. I try to keep the relief off my face and somehow end up crinkling my nose.

"Yes, it's gross," Rubin agrees with me, tossing the lime on the table. "The peel is not good to eat."

"Well, maybe if you'd give us something to eat," Andrew mutters, as if he's bitter and his belly isn't full.

Damn. He's a good actor. I bet he'd be great at sex role play. My lady bits agree, reminding me that I haven't had an orgasm since yesterday. That's the longest I've gone on this island without one.

Suity sneers down at me. "She sign papers, you get food."

I turn to the twins. "Are you really gonna let this asshole deprive me of food? You gonna let him speak to your future wife this way?" My sentence is too long. It's taking too long for comprehension to dawn. I dumb it down. "Marriage papers? Me? Punch him."

Rubin and Reval look at each other and bite their lips. They look torn about what to do. Ugh. Part of me loves that they kind of want to obey my order. And part of me hates that they're stupid enough to think that might be a good idea.

Rubin does turn to Suity. "You'd do well not to ..." he trails off but gestures at me.

It's a start. Given the fact that he's a pussy, those are practically fighting words from Rubin.

Suity is not torn up about being a jerk. He seems to embrace it. He pulls the lime off the table and drops it. He kicks the lime at me and says, "If you're hungry, go ahead. Eat. I will watch."

Dammit all to hell. Mother fucker. I don't want to eat this fucking lime. I want to kick it away. But that will just start shit up. Ok, focus. I don't want them to stay here. Right now, I just want to go back to grating limes in peace. I want Jeremiah to finish this damn bomb so we can attack.

I need to figure out something that will keep them away from the guys and out of the kitchen for a couple of hours. I rack my brain as I slowly pick up the lime and press it to my lips, trying to act compliant and gain the twins' sympathy. I bite into it and juice squirts all over me. My toes curl at the combination of bitter and sour and utter nastiness. It kind of reminds me of Shane Paul's spunk.

Spunk. That does give me an idea. And idea for something I can do, something Jeremiah and the other guys can't. Something important. I swallow down the nasty lime juice and try to think of how to word this properly. I have to be convincing. I have to make them think I'm telling the truth. That I care and shit and this isn't just a ploy. The twins.

The twins are the key. Betraying motherfuckers. But they're weak. Mushy and shit. They think our skin-to-skin contact means something more than a quick O. If I want to see them fly sky high, I need Andrew and company to finish that fucking bomb.

I eye Rubin and Reval, the hot-as-sin fakers. I'm gonna have to get the others to follow along, but I need to bait this hook. My eyes lock on Rubin. And I turn on seductive voice, like I'm tuning into the old Delilah show on the radio. "I'm hungry ... but not just for food. I haven't had an orgasm since yesterday." Orgasm is a word I know these assholes know. I taught it to them.

Immediately, Rubin's eyes light up. "You want help?"

I lick my lips so that I don't laugh at how easy his interest sparks. Distracting them and getting them out of here might be easier than I thought. "Yes, my fingers can't reach deep enough. I need dick."

Blob turns to the other guys. "I feel like this is not real."

I turn around and ask Rubin and Reval. "Have you told him about your orgasm board?"

The twins started an orgasm board the first time we had sex. It's a scoreboard they keep posted in the living room of their villa. They've been having a competition to see who could give me more orgasms. It's part of why they've gotten to stick around so long on this goddamn island.

"Tell this guy about the time you gave me ten orgasms in one sitting," I urge the twins. "How you used the shower sprayer—"

"Shower?" Blob asks.

"Yes, and tongues, and vibrators, and the double team ..." Rubin and Reval are pitching tents through their pants at my words. "You guys have made me addicted to dick."

The twins swell up with pride. Literally swell. Rubin, I think he might be the slightly dimmer one, takes a step toward me. But Suity grabs his shoulder.

An argument in Russian erupts. Broken English phrases shoot out of the twins' mouths. "Is true!" and "Tiger style!" and "Full train, six guys, one night." That makes Blob and Suity go quiet for a second. When Reval mentions the double facial, they all turn and stare at me for a second.

"No," Blob shakes his head. "No woman does this."

I raise an eyebrow and nod, giving him a naughty little grin. "I love facials." Total fucking lie. But—whatever it takes. I need to get these guys out of here. I need to get them to fuck me like I used to get those dickwads at the sex club to fuck me to make Shane Paul jealous. Only this time, my goal's bigger. I'm gonna fuck them so that we can kill them.

The argument starts up again and the Russians form a huddle. While they're turned away, I shove the chloroform rag from under my ass to under the table, in case this crazy stunt works out. I can't tell, but I fucking hope my pity facial is pushing me toward the win.

While the Russians argue, I make eye contact with the other three guys who are tied up. I mouth to Andrew, "I'm going to try and get them out of here and keep them distracted." In case he's not sure what I mean, I add, "with sex."

Andrew rolls his eyes and nods. "Obviously," he mouths back.

"You okay with that?" I mean, I kinda already started down this path, but shit. I don't wanna hurt Andrew. Or piss him off.

He mimes a silent explosion with his mouth and hands and then winks.

Fuck yeah. I love how we're always on the same page. I wink back.

I think the facial thing might have made Blob interested, at least. I just need to push them over the edge, so to speak. I reach down my body. The ropes don't have a ton of slack, but I'm able to pinch my nipples. Reval stops talking first. Then Blob turns to look at me. When Rubin turns, I leave one hand on my breasts and lift my free hand to my mouth. I swirl my pointer finger around my tongue. Then I drag it back down my chest and trace the other nipple. I groan.

Suity and J2 finally cave and looks at me. I pinch my nipples, tugging on them, enjoying the sensation of having all eyes in the room on me. I've always loved attention. I love the ability to drive men wild. My chest fills with that wanton rush of sexual power—their desire—as my hands wander down my belly. I part my legs and let the Russians stare at my gaping slit. I pull aside the lips, letting them see the rosy center. Then I start sliding my fingers up and down along the sides, teasing myself, but not going right for the clit. I close my eyes and throw my head back, playing it up more than I really feel it. "Rubin. Reval. I need you. And your friends. I need it. Have to have sex."

There's more arguing in Russian. But it's low and frantic,

not loud like before. I start moving my hand faster and the arguing sputters out to grumbles and then murmurs and then nothing. I hear a footstep on the tile floor come closer to me. The smile that stretches across my face has nothing to do with my impending orgasm. It has to do with the fact that I'm about to win.

CHAPTER THIRTEEN

KATIE

We hike down, dragging Peter Brown with us. He protests at first, but then we remind him there's a doctor on the island—Andrew. Since he's grunting and groaning with every step from the damned bites and can hardly twist, (he's seriously as swollen as a misshapen balloon) he shuts up. He hangs at the back of the group with Alec, who has undone enough of Sports Coat's legs for the guy to walk, but keeps an arm threateningly on the other guy's shoulder, gun in hand—just in case.

Kenneth, Danny, and I discuss how the hell we might take out the remaining gangsters and the two backstabbing twins. My three guys, a limping and reluctant Peter Brown and a prisoner against potentially seven dudes. And while the twins didn't come to the island with weapons, we have to assume the other five are armed. They might have even brought guns for the twins.

"The good news is they don't seem to have vests on," Kenneth points out. "So our guns have just as good a chance as theirs."

I worry my lip, which makes it start to bleed. It's been rather abused lately. "We need something better than guns. We need to be able to take out more than one of them at a time."

Danny runs a hand through his blond hair, his tricep gleaming in the afternoon light. "I might be able to help. I did a stint for a hypnotist—"

I hold up a hand. "Not now. Please." I turn away from Danny. I know he can't help it. But I can't believe he's lying now. We need a plan! We need an idea. Something real that might work to take these guys down. Right now I'm as nervous as a cat stuck in a roomful of rocking chairs. Those Russians are the real deal.

Danny doesn't drop the hypnotist thing though. "But, he did this thing where he—" Danny just can't help himself. He can't stop the lies from pouring out.

I put my fist to my forehead in frustration. "Stop lying."

"I'm not!" Danny grabs my hand off my forehead. He pulls it down and entwines our fingers. "I swear to God, I'm not lying, Katie." His eyes shine earnestly.

"Even if you aren't, hypnotism isn't real," Kenneth scoffs, rolling his eyes.

"Let me try it on our POW," Danny points at Sports Coat.

"We don't have time."

"Two minutes. Just two minutes."

Alec calls out from the back. "We'll probably need to break in a couple hours to pee. Just let him do it then."

Why he says that, I have no clue. Probably to keep the

peace so Kenneth and Danny don't chip at one another for the next few hours. I guess that's worth the two minutes of wasted effort. I roll my eyes. "Fine."

Danny grins and fist pumps. Then he lifts our entwined fingers and kisses my hand. "You'll see. I'm gonna make that Russian think he's on our side."

I shake my head while Kenneth and I continue talking about possibilities based on what I've got available in my villa. The conversation goes on for awhile. An hour, maybe two. My throat is parched by the time we start repeating suggestions we've already made. Luring the Russians out one by one seems like our best option. But, the likelihood of getting more than one of them out and down before the others all come chasing after us seems slim.

"We need some kind of distraction. Like a fire or something," Kenneth says.

"It's too wet here," Alec calls out. "Stuff will smoke but not really burn."

"We could smoke them out," I say. "I mean, you know, start a fire somewhere to drive them where we want them."

"The golf course is pretty narrow," Danny contributes. "If we stay in the trees—"

"Still a ton of directions they can go," Alec says from behind us.

We argue for a good chunk of the hike. Other than Alec, none of us have ever really faced off against men who're meaner than a box of snakes. And anytime Alec did it, he had a whole jet fulla' bombs.

"Well, we could just collect mangoes and let Danny hit them at their heads," I joke. "Those fucking monkeys nearly brained me that way."

To my surprise, the guys all stop and stare. "That's actually not a bad idea. Smoke them out and then maybe, two guns and Danny with a racquet ..."

Alec asks Danny, "What's your serve speed?"

"One fifty."

I yank Danny by the hand. He's refused to let go of me, even though our palms are slick with sweat. "I'm sorry. I don't know tennis. I was half joking. What's that?"

He grins down at me. And it's a panty-evaporating, proud-as-a-peacock grin. "A hundred fifty miles per hour, Katie."

"Shut the front door. You're lying."

He shakes his head. "Nope."

My eyes trace his huge biceps and my nipples tighten. "I had no idea you were that strong," I murmur.

"All for you."

"Lie!" Kenneth calls out from the side.

"Hey, don't be a clamjam," Danny spouts back, good-naturedly though.

"A what?"

"A crotch nazi."

"Oh my God. We don't have time for more sex right now," Kenneth growls, stomping on ahead. "In case you haven't noticed, we are stranded on a deserted island with no fucking food and a bunch of psychos." He tromps down the path, putting some distance between our group and himself.

I glance back at Alec, who just shakes his head. "Give him a minute."

"Maybe it's time for us to take a break," Danny says.

Alec agrees. Peter Brown sighs and immediately sits down on the path, right where he was standing, no preamble whatsoever.

Alec unwraps even more of the twine on Sports Coat, revealing the man's waist. Our POW clearly pissed himself at some point. Great. Alec sighs and shakes his head, and leads the man off to let him do his business.

This leaves me and Danny essentially alone together. Danny looks down at me and opens his mouth, but then his gaze flickers over to Peter Brown. "Um ... we need a minute."

"Not gonna fuck in front of me like the other guy?" Peter scoffs. "Trust me, I'm used to it by now."

"You were turned around. So you don't even know what happened."

"Bullshit. She was screaming like a—"

My cheeks go scarlet.

"Do *not* finish that sentence," Danny growls.

Peter just glares sullenly and stays in his spot.

Danny shakes his head and leads me a bit away so we can't be overheard.

"Sorry about that."

I wave it off. "Peter's always been a scumball. You okay?"

Danny looks down. He unclasps our hands and runs his hands over my shoulders and down my arms. He swallows hard and repeats the gesture, like he's nervous or something.

His nerves make me laugh nervously.

Then he laughs. A snort slips out.

That makes me laugh a little harder.

We end up laughing hard, at nothing—deep belly-wrenching, rib-aching laughter at nothing. I have to swipe tears away. When we finally get control of ourselves, Danny reaches out and gives my hand a squeeze. My eyes connect with him and his face is suddenly far too serious for the moment we just had.

He swallows hard and then says slowly, "Katie, I don't want this to end. If we get out of this... I don't want this to— " His hand gestures between the two of us before he drops my hand and stares at the forest floor. "I know for you it's just fuck buddies. But I have never laughed this much with anyone else my entire life. I've never had someone call me on my bullshit and not hate me for it. I've never felt—" he cuts himself off, scared to continue.

My head doesn't know what to think, but my heart is very fucking clear on the matter. I grab back Danny's hand. I have to choke back a sob. I have to fight my skepticism. Because there's no way Danny and the other guys should mean this much to me this quickly. But they do. And I'm older. Technically, I'm the grown-up here. I should be able to articulate what I feel better than some twenty-four-year-old. But my lips don't cooperate. All I can get out is a bumbling, "Me too."

Danny's arms wrap around me in a bear hug that's so tight I can hardly breathe. And it's as perfect as a summer day, as Cinderella's shoe, as a shutout baseball game. We fit together, Danny and me. And when I hug him, I know I'm where I belong.

DANNY'S hypnotic abilities suck way worse than his hugs. Way, way worse.

We untie Sports Coat. Alec trains a gun on the Russian as Danny dangles a rock tied to a string in front of the foreigner's face.

"You'll fight with us," Danny intones.

"Shouldn't you choose a better turn of phrase? Fighting with us can mean fighting us," Kenneth snarks from his spot leaning against a tree. He's gotten progressively more grumpy throughout the afternoon. And he won't say why, even though I asked. He just runs his hands over his dark hair and squints off into the distance. He does that now, rolling his eyes at Danny's poor choice of words.

Danny's face turns red and he changes the phrase he's chanting to, "You'll change sides and fight against the other Russians. You'll fight alongside us. You'll fight alongside us."

Peter Brown snorts in the background. Apparently, everyone's a skeptic.

I don't feel like this is going particularly well, but Danny's trying to help. So I press my lips together and bite my tongue.

Three minutes later, I'm near my breaking point. Danny's been doing the same damn thing the entire time and it doesn't look like anything's happening. I'm about to tell Danny thanks for trying when he changes his tone.

"Stand up," Danny commands, switching from his muttering chant to a loud, booming voice.

Sports Coat stands.

All of us exchange a startled look. What the fuck? The guy doesn't even speak English. How did he know to stand up? Either he lied, or the hypnotism worked.

Danny looks completely and utterly awed. He glances over at Kenneth and says, "Not too shabby, huh?"

He uses his commanding voice again. "Hold out your left hand."

Sports Coat starts to extend his left hand. And my jaw drops.

But then Sports Coat smacks Danny across the face and books it into the trees.

Alec's the first to recover, leaping over a bush to chase the foreigner.

"Fuck!" Danny pulls at his hair. I grab his hand and yank him along. Once I'm sure Danny, Kenneth, and Peter

Brown are following, I let go of Danny as I try to hurry after the fucking-liar-face Russian. He's totally not Sports Coat anymore. He's Liar-face. Maybe even Shane Paul the second. Fucktard.

Shane Paul II trips and I hear a "Ohh sheet!" The lying liar even curses in English!

"STOP!" Alec yells. He stops running, his eyes down. He puts his hand out like a barrier, physically warning us all to stop.

I slow down and come to stand beside Alec. The forest falls away suddenly. The ground just cuts off, like a knife sliced down through the island and cut off a sliver. I cautiously move toward the edge and peer over. At the very bottom, at least fifty feet down, waves crash against the cliff. A shiver runs down my spine. I'm about to go full southerner and say "Bless his soul," when I spot Shane Paul II perched on a narrow ledge halfway down the cliff.

"What the hell? What are the chances?"

Alec and the guys stand beside me and peer down.

Kenneth whistles. "He's one lucky fuck."

That lucky fuck screams up at us, "Pool me up!"

I want to fucking yell back down at him, "Don't speak English, huh?"

Alec is the first to straighten. "I vote we leave him there."

"What?" I'm startled. I look up to see his unforgiving brown eyes.

"Not forever. But we don't have to watch our backs and

worry about him if he's there. We take out the others, we can come fish him out and throw him in whatever jail we make for them."

He's sugar-coating it for me. I can tell. But I need that. I can't take too much more right now. And he's right. We need to be able to focus on Heather. We need our full attention on distracting and taking out those other Russians. At best, this Shane Paul fucker would slow us down. At worst ... I can't even think about it. "Alright."

"Good plan. Far as I'm concerned, we can leave the fucker here forever," Kenneth spits, then turns around and stomps back through the trees.

We look at Peter Brown, who shrugs, like the slimy bastard he is. "Better odds with him there." He follows Kenneth.

"Danny?" I ask and turn to search his eyes.

He's not looking at me though. I'm not even sure he heard our conversation. Danny is staring out at the waves, which are lit in blinding bands by the afternoon sun.

"Do you see that?" he asks. He lifts his finger and I squint, trying to find what he's staring at in the patchwork of blue.

It takes a minute, but there, coming close to the cliff, is a little boat. Two men are on it, one of them steering, the other holding tight to a suitcase. I squint. "Is that ... Anthony Drake?!"

The sun glints off the reporter's hair suddenly, like the universe is answering me.

"Looks like it," Alec grunts. "How the fuck did he get a call out when we can't?"

"He must have done it last night, before the Russians blocked the signal," I say.

"And the gangsters didn't hear this fucking boat? Didn't find Drake?"

I shrug. "They didn't find us. Maybe they're not the brightest. I hope they aren't. Or maybe they're distracted—" Thoughts of the things they could be distracted by make bile rise in my throat. I can't bear the thought of Heather getting tortured.

Danny's quiet as we watch the boat head away. It's like watching hope smile at you, then flip you off, flounce her skirt, and walk away. Hope was the bitch that ruled my high school.

We watch the boat head toward another island. From our vantage point, it seems like it's only a stone's throw away.

"How far is that island, do you think?" Danny suddenly asks.

"Nine, ten miles," Alec replies.

"I could do that," Danny says, his voice pitched low and thoughtful.

"What?" I jerk my head up and search his face.

"I could swim that."

I feel like someone punched me in the gut. "Through open ocean? Are you insane? There's waves and sharks and currents and I-don't-even-fucking-know-what." That idea's crazier than a mule chewing on a bumblebee.

Danny turns and looks at Alec, avoiding my gaze. "I think I can make it. I was on swim team in high school."

"Lie!" I shout as that punch to the gut turns into a tire iron smashing into me. He's serious. I grab onto Danny's arm and yank him back, away from the edge of the cliff. Clearly, he's got vertigo. He isn't thinking straight. This is nuts.

"They'll have a phone there," Danny says; he still doesn't look at me. He and Alec seem to have a silent conversation. And it freaks me the fuck out.

After I've got Danny back from the cliff-edge, I go and grab Alec. I try to move him, but he won't budge. He does break off from staring at Danny to look over at the other island again. "It's risky."

Danny shakes his head. "It's not any worse than what we've already talked about. It's better than hitting fucking mangoes at those assholes when you all have guns. I want to actually do something worth a shit. And this way, it's only risking me."

Everything in me grinds to a halt. I don't think my heart is still beating. I turn to Danny, aghast. "What!? No!" I run to him and toss my arms around his waist. "You're not going. You can't. I'm not gonna let you."

Alec squints at the waves for a long time. Finally, he turns back to Danny. He nods once.

"NO!!!!" I scream.

Danny puts his arms around me and gives me a hug. I clutch at him. He tries to slip out of my arms but I claw at him, trying to draw him closer. "You can't. You can't."

"I have to. It's the best way," he whispers into my hair. He kisses the top of my head and I feel that kiss through my entire body, like I've been drenched in a rainstorm made of the tears that come from lost wishes and dead dreams. I sputter, "But, but you said …" He wanted an after. Why the fuck is he doing this if he wants an after? "Don't!"

Alec's hard hands yank me away from Danny. Alec wraps his arms around me. I buck and fight. I scream, "Don't you dare, Danny! Don't you dare!"

He gives me a regretful, sad-puppy eyes look for a second. And my heart breaks. It turns inside out, like an umbrella in a storm—twisted, deformed, mangled.

Danny says, "I have to try."

Then he turns on his heel and my liar, my precious liar, walks away.

CHAPTER FOURTEEN

HEATHER

I grab Rubin and Reval's hands and lead them out of the kitchen. Suity and Blob follow behind. J2 is the last out of the kitchen, and of course, he has to make an asshole comment. "No way she can take on five."

I drop the twins' hands. Because that right there, is a fucking insult. And he might be a killer Russian mobster, but if there is one thing that I perfected during my swinger years with that limp dick Shane Paul, it's group sex. I'm a blow queen. An orgmist. I'm a beastmaster at the sex circus. A spank bank with enough gold to break your piggy and make him 'wee wee' all the way home. I whip around and point at J2. My eyes are lasers when they land on him and size him up. "Buddy, I've been a part of more orgies than you've ever even watched on your pathetic Soviet-era black and white TV." I have no idea if that's what J2 has, but fuck him, I'm so mad that I don't care if my insults make sense. I stomp over and shove my finger right into his Adonis-like chest. "I'm the goddamn Batman of sex. I've got all the fun toys and I know how to use them. Mouth, pussy, ass, and two hands. That's five things right there. Or don't you know how to count?" I reach down and grab him by the dick through his pants.

He stares down at me, his hazel eyes hard and angry in a way that gets me hot and bothered. But the sneer on his face and the clench of his jaw show me he's not amused. "Batman is man."

"Batman is the best."

"Because he's man."

Ohh, he did not just say that. J2 is not arguing sexist shit with me. I bear down on his dick, squeezing hard. That's not my brightest moment, because J2 whips out his gun and cocks it. He presses it against my temple and my mouth has to swallow my heart back down because it tries to jump ship. Oh crap. Now I gotta undo the mess I made. Fuck. Luckily my tits tend to help earn forgiveness whenever someone's decided my mouth's earned a beat-down.

I pretend to ignore the gun as I unzip J2's pants and pull his dick out. I pretend to ignore the fact that underneath the pressed pants he's wearing, he's got on tighty whities that are worn paper thin. Guess gangstering doesn't pay so well. No wonder they want my money. I bend forward over his cock, trying not to let my fingers tremble. Goddamned automatic nervous system. *Remember, Heath, this is a sport. Orgasms are just another goal, another score. No big deal. You're gonna rack up such a big fucking score, girl,* I tell myself. *You're gonna smack down these dimwits.* That's right. They won't even know what hit them. I lean forward

slowly, making sure the other guys get a good view of
my ass.

I'll need the others to come to my rescue if J2 gets pissy. So
I'd best give them a show. I spread my legs apart, so that my
slit gapes. And then I arch my back so they can see it as I
lean over J2's dick.

I spit on his shaft and use my hands to lube it up. Then I
jerk it gently for a few tugs, and either J2 realizes that I'm
not trying to kill him or he realizes that I have the power to
destroy him because his cock's in my hands. If he guessed
the latter, he'd be correct. He's got the gun, I've got the cock.
It's total mutual-assured destruction.

After a few more strokes, J2 uncocks his gun and holds it
limp at his side. I'm so, so tempted to try and knock it away
from him like I did with Suity earlier. But that's not the
plan. I need to stick to the plan. We need to blow all these
fuckers to bits. Not in a sex way. And we're only gonna be
able to do that if we build a coo-coo-banana-loco, fool bomb
outta limes. I stand up suddenly, keeping J2's dick in my
hands as I turn around. I face the others, still stroking him.

"Come on," I order. "My villa's got condoms. And all the
lube we need."

Blob, his paunch highly visible now that he's lost his jacket,
leans over and says to Suity, "I knew the sexy times was
true."

He crosses his arms above his belly and rests them there. I
see pit stains from sweat on his shirt. I have to look away
before I talk myself out of a sixsome.

I stride past them, kind of enjoying the fact that J2 is stumbling along behind me since I've still got a grip on his dick. He trips over his pants, which are still stuck around his ankles. "Stop. Wait."

I just pretend I don't understand him. I mean, turnabout and all that since they didn't bother to learn fucking English properly. "I am hurrying! Geez! Anxious much?" I tell him, biting down on my grin.

After another stumble, he grabs my wrist and forces my hand off his dick. I consider scratching him when he does that, but ... I need to keep these foreign dickheads occupied for a couple hours. And his dickhead won't last if I give it a boo boo. Men are weak like that. So, I let him go.

Dammit. I roll my eyes before turning back to the group. Because I know there's nothing that turns a lot of guys on more than pretending to be an innocent little ditz, I make my eyes wide to double the dumb-factor. "Oh, no. Five big strong men are after me? What are they gonna do to me?" I let out this obnoxious squeak I've perfected over the years. I think it sounds like a fucking dying rabbit. But it seems to perk up the idiotic male predator in most men. Yeesh.

I back away, looking side to side, like some porn-star D-list actress. I make sure to clasp my hands under my boobs to give them some pop. The twins eat that shit right up. Even J2 seems into it after he gets his pants back up.

Then I turn and run, making sure to put in a little extra bounce so they can see my tits flop. They take off after me. I swear—making men horny is a dead cinch. I run out the doors of my kitchen and past the pool. The place is a dead zone. There's nobody here, other than the damned incessant parrots who're squawking "Get the fuck out. You tryna' cheat me?" Part of me wonders what the hell they'll squawk after I leave. I hope it's "Oh, yeah right there, baby!" and not, "Don't Shoot!"

Damn, it's like a sauna outside. Even though the path to my villa's not too far, and even though I make the elliptical my bitch, the mid-afternoon heat is killer. Sweat is dripping down my neck and between my breasts. I take the turn down the path to my villa—the large white palace that was a monument to orgasmic bliss before now—only to find the fuckers broke down my front door at some point. It's splintered and it looks like it's been kicked to death. The bottom two feet hang down at an angle. Goddamned motherfuckers! I paid a security deposit on this place. That shit ain't cheap. Broken door or no, the guys are catching up. I try to shove that broken hunk of wood shut in their faces.

"No! No! You can't have me!" I call out in my ditz-girl voice. "I'm a virgin! I'm saving myself for true love!"

The twins burst down the door and back me into the living room with, wolf-like grins on their faces. They've done this play-acting shit with me for awhile. They snap into character. "What do you mean? We love you. It is true. We'll marry you."

And ... they killed it. The thought of marriage brings me right back to reality. Marry one of those fucks or get shot in the face. That is ... if their daddy realizes the helicopter's broken and comes to rescue his wittle bitty pwincesses.

"New game!" I stand stock still and glare at all of them, summoning up my dominatrix persona.

The twins freeze immediately. They're used to the quick

changes of pace I pull. But Blob's too busy wheezing to care and Suity and J2 are back by the broken doorway, arguing about who's gonna hold the three guns and stand guard while the other one gets to participate. Paranoid much? There's no one else here and the guys are "tied" up.

I hold up my hand to stop the twins from coming any closer. "Shirts off," I command in a sultry voice.

The twins obey and unfortunately, so does Blob. He does not have the gorgeous thick pecs that they do. In fact, he's got very hairy, very puffy nipples. They look like they belong on the end of a baby bottle they're so big.

My gag reflex sends my gaze elsewhere. I end up looking back at Suity and J2 to see who's joining nekked time. I realize that they've gone the mature route of rock-paper-scissors-slap in order to decide. They play three rounds, and the winner of each round gets to slap the other man in the face. Best out of three wins. Suity wins.

J2 takes his red cheeks and all the guns and plops grumpily into a chair to watch. He curses. Some kinda, "Sooka shinananakala," weirdness that I don't understand. I don't even think those are letters he's saying.

"Shirt off!" I command the others. "Kneel!"

I don't know if Suity understands me, or just is ready to get undressed, but he shucks his clothes. Unlike my puppy-pal twins, he doesn't stop with his shirt. He peels off his pants, too. And damn, the man is hung. He's pretty hot, too, if you like them pale. Not my usual go-to. But I can deal. Until I see that Blob follows Suity's lead instead of my directions. Chubs drops his pants.

I clench my fists.

I look down at the twins. "Good boys." They grin at my praise. Damn they're hot. That's the redeeming factor in this bullshit show I'm putting on. I inhale sharply, like I'm pissed. My hand flies out and I point an accusatory finger at Suity and Blob. "Now, go spank them. Remind them who they're supposed to listen to."

Dammit all. It's a sight to see when R&R stand and go over to those other men. They push them roughly toward the couch. Blob and Suity protest, arguing in Russian. But the twins give curt responses as they bend the other two men over the couch and smack their asses. Hell yeah! I am about to crow. I'm about to scream in mirth. But I can't. Dammit all. This dominatrix shit is hard work. I have to bite down on my lips really, really hard.

But then I make eye contact with J2. He's cracking up. I have to turn around for a second, blow out a monster breath to get control of myself, and then turn back around to watch. Because, hell no, I ain't missing all that.

After a couple smacks, the twins look up at me for direction. Suity just stands up and glares, covering his ass and shouldering past the twins so he can stand at the back of the group. Yeah, that's right buddy. You should be embarrassed. You were a bad boy. I shake my head at him, pretending to be disappointed.

He scratches the side of his head in a way that makes me kind of wonder if he's calling me crazy. But he doesn't loop his fingers all big, so I decide to let it go and not punish him further.

Of course, watching Suity means I took my eyes off Blob. Suddenly, his naked dick is swinging right in my personal space. He's got a grin on his face. He doesn't seem to be pissed about the spanking. His little red monster is bobbing proudly (emphasis on the little).

Aw crap. Time for a new game. I deliberately push Blob aside, saying, "You're not first."

Blob's about to grab at me when I reach out for Suity. I've figured out this little group dynamic. And while I think J2 is the true Alpha, Suity McGunpants is second. I run my hand down Suity's pecs. Oh shit, those are nice. So are his abs. He tenses them under my fingers to make them even more defined and I feel myself getting a little turned on as I trace each one. My nipples pebble. Damn. At some point, if I have to ride someone ... his yum factor might just persuade me.

But, business, I remind myself. *You're here to draw this shit out, and keep them occupied.*

Nothing keeps a guy's brain more occupied than having someone touch his dick. But ... I can't let this go quickly. I have no idea what their stamina is like. Ohhh, that reminds me of a group activity I did with some of the harem guys a few days ago. I smile to myself as I bend forward and pretend I'm gonna put my mouth on Suity's swollen shaft. Instead, I tease, sticking out my tongue and waggling it, staying just out of reach. I shoot my right arm straight out, palm up. "Cock ring!" I command.

And like the little bitches they are, those twinsies hop to and grab a new cock ring out of the organized little basket of toys—thanks to Katie—that sit on my dining table. One of them places a ring in my hand. I don't even look to see which one, because I'm not gonna thank them.

I give Suity a smile as I slide that ring down his shaft and then press a surprise button on the side. The cock ring lights up bright red and starts vibrating against his shaft and balls. Suity practically jumps at the sensation. But I just smile wide. "This here is called a hummdinger. We had a little competition in the harem a few days ago to see how many hummdingers the guys could stand before they shot their loads. Bet they've got you beat," I say as I stroke him a few times.

Suity tenses when I use my fingers to circle the sensitive head of his dick. There's already precum. No way he's gonna hold out longer than the twins.

When he realizes I'm just smearing the precum around and not gonna spank him or something else, he relaxes and leans into my touch. That's right, buddy. You're putty in my hands. He's no longer staring at me in a pissed way. I can see the lust; his eyes grow hooded as that vibrator makes his balls wobble more than a grandma's bingo wings.

This is too fucking easy.

"Dicks out!" I use my drill sergeant voice.

Even though they're the ones with the guns, every single one of them complies, even J2 whips down his pants to play. I don't even bother to hide my smile this time. Male ego plus male sex drive equals Heather's a winner.

"Spit and lube up. I'm gonna put as many cock rings as I can on each of your dicks. Whoever can stand the most rings for the longest amount of time, gets to go first next round."

The twins immediately follow my command.

Blob stares down, and looks a little dejected. I know why. We'll be lucky if we can fit three rings on that thing. Sucks to be him. I decide I'm gonna do what I can to avoid riding that pinkie finger.

I gather up a handful of cock rings and roll one down each dick.

Blob doesn't even make it to the next round before he spurts. Whoops.

I use my hand and cover my mouth to keep from laughing out loud. Blob doesn't even clean up the floor he jizzed on. He just goes and collapses on my couch, naked. His head falls back in that empty, dazed post-orgasm-about-to-sleep way. I send him good dream vibes, cause hey—all the easier for me.

One down. Hopefully, Blobby likes long naps.

I get through one more round before Suity squirts. Dammit! I check the clock. It hasn't even been five minutes! What the hell? Hasn't the man ever heard of edging? Has he ever given a woman an orgasm in her entire life? I mean, I couldn't even get a single orgasm out of five minutes! Shit!

Suity leans against the back of the couch panting, while the twins and J2 exchange smug looks with each other. I dunno while they're all feeling so superior. I'm the one getting my captors off without actually fucking them. Plus, their dicks look like ridiculous little railroad crossing gates right now. Their levers bob up and down while flashing red lights

scream, "Warning, Heather! Freight train's cumming down the track!" I kind of have the urge to grab some eyeshadow and stripe their dicks in black and white to finish off the look, but I don't think they'd let me go that far. I'm surprised as hell they've let me get away with this.

I bet not one of them besides the twins has ever been in an orgy before. Which is just sad. Sex is supposed to be fun. Too many people let it get all sappy dappy and ruin a good time.

I toss on another ring and J2 tenses. The twins just frown, their foreheads wrinkling in concentration. I can practically hear their thoughts: snow, math, and sports stats.

For a second, I'm pretty fucking proud, maybe even a bit smug about the twins. When they came here, yeah, they were good. But now, they can keep four cock rings on no problem. And I've made them work on their stamina. Just thinking about how I made them work on it—my mind flashes over all the positions and workouts I've put them through—gets me hot and bothered. My pussy gets a bit riled up.

Mama might need to get a little bit of action at some point. I fan myself and walk over to get a better look at J2. His face is practically turning purple with the strain. I lean forward more and blow lightly on the tip of his dick, trying to tease him into delirium. I wonder if I could maybe sneak over and grab a gun—but his hand closes around the handle of the nearest revolver and his grip tightens as he sprays all over his own stomach.

I jut my lip out. "Awww, I was hoping you'd be first next round."

He grins. "I will." He gestures behind me and I see, to my shock, both twins have come.

"What the hell boys? I trained you better than that!"

"You bent over his cock," Reval pants.

I shake my head, disgusted at both of them. "Fifteen push ups!"

J2 laughs when they comply. "You would make very good in military, I think."

I shrug and pat his back, which turns into stroking the muscles there and caressing his triceps. Fucking shit. I've never fucked a Schwartzenegger-wannabe before. There aren't that many in Oklahoma. It's more of a fast-food and meth kinda place than a haven for body builders.

I let my hands wander further. Yum. Just touching him has me clenching my teeth and other bits in anticipation. I lean in and whisper into his ear. "When you've recovered, let me know." I lean forward and drag my nipples gently up and down the outside of his arm.

Even though the twins have just come, they groan at the sight.

I let my hands and body wander up and down J2's body, drawing it out. Eventually, I start to use him like a stripper pole, dancing on him. I end up tossing a leg up on his shoulders, hooking my foot behind his head, and then leaning back slowly.

"Shit!"

I see Suity spurt as I hang upside down. I slowly pull myself up and laugh. He's already come a second time! Unbeliev-

able. I look up, expecting J2 to laugh with me, but he's got a hot look in his eyes. Oh, hell yes. I'm revved up and ready.

I turn to the twins. "Condom?" They groan again. That is one of their favorite words. They've gone through three big boxes of them since we've been here.

I kind of expected them to grab the condom out of the box on my entry table. But, I'm not surprised when one of the twins—I think it's Reval—rifles through his pants on the floor and pulls a condom out of his pocket. Even though they were naked in the pool area with me yesterday, even though I've been tied up in the kitchen all morning, it does not surprise me at all that Rubin and Reval got dressed, but also got sex ready, just in case. Those men are sex ready at all times. If only they were as prepared in other areas of life. But I use their sex-crazed minds to my advantage. I snatch the foil packet out of Reval's hand and rip it open. I spit on my hand and rub down J2's shaft.

Suddenly Suity's at J2's side, his own staff sheathed even though he's nowhere close to ready for action. It kind of feels like he's lining up to ensure he's next. That thought makes me laugh. Because I decide who's next.

I completely ignore him and grab J2's hand, shoving it onto my breast. I show him exactly how to play with my nipple before I make him switch. I call out, "Heated nipple clamps!"

The twins hand over the clamps, which attach to a little battery pack. I switch it on. Then I open the clamps.

"Fuck yes," J2 whispers.

He shrieks when I snap the clamp onto his nipple. Why, I'm

not sure. Maybe I should have warned him? But trust me, nipple clamps feel fucking good. I smack his hands away when he tries to pull the clamp off.

"I know what the hell I'm doing!" I tell him.

He rips the clamp off anyway and tosses it to the side. He comes forward and grabs me. He picks me up and shoves me down onto his shaft while he's still standing. Fucking yes! Lightning crawls up my spine and I tilt my head back. He dips his head and takes my nipple in his mouth and starts sucking. He walks me over to the wall and shoves me up against it, hard.

Then he rails me, holding my ass with one hand and sliding the other in front of me so my clit hits it every time I bounce.

The twins stroke off to the sight of us, and Suity starts to get hard.

J2 starts grunting. Less than a minute later, he groans. I wrench his nipples and twist as he does, drawing out his orgasm.

He stops, and pushes me into the wall with his hips as he pants. "I cannot believe you twisted."

I smack his shoulder. "Next time, you'll let me clamp them."

He gives a small, tired nod and wipes a bead of sweat from his forehead. He drops me and I pinch my own nipples as I think—still trying to give Suity and the twins a show.

To say I'm disappointed in J2 is an understatement. There was no robot-level endurance in his performance. But ... besides that, I mean, what we did could hardly be called sex. I look up at the clock that hangs in my living room. It hasn't even been forty minutes since we left the kitchen! And I haven't even come once! All these fuckers are on their third or fourth round.

I'm supposed to draw this shit out for hours. When Suity spurts seconds later just from staring at my tits, I realize just how much of an uphill battle I've got ahead of me.

CHAPTER FIFTEEN

KATIE

For the first hour, Alec carries me while I sob. He tries to set me down once or twice, but when I try to run off through the trees to find Danny and stop him, Alec resorts to holding me pressed against his chest. His suit jacket gets soaked, and I'm not sure if it's from my tears or from the effort of carrying me through the afternoon heat. Eventually, I calm down enough to walk on my own. But the ache in my chest doesn't let up—it hurts so bad that I think dying might hurt less. The fear for someone else, for someone you care about ... that's worse than death. It's a kind of pain that eats and gnaws at you, like your insides are full of gleaming orange coals that burn away your very spirit.

I've been scared for Heather. But I don't think anything that's happened feels as real as this. I haven't seen her face. I've imagined her suffering. But I haven't seen. And imagination versus the moment Danny walked away, determined to find a beach and wade into that water because he thought that was the best option for us ... Fucking hell. It's the noblest, stupidest, most awful thing I've ever lived through. And yet ... it makes me love him all the more. I love Danny.

I know I shouldn't. Logically, it doesn't make sense. He's too young. He's a fucking liar. We hardly know each other. But he's sweet and funny and selfless. So selfless. And all my logic just fades away when my mind conjures up his face. Heather's always said love erases your brain and makes you a bumble butt. I always laughed at that saying. She used to say that about herself and Shane Paul every time she took him back. I guess it's true. For me and Danny both. Him, for being stupid enough to throw himself in the ocean on the off-chance he survives, me for loving him all the more for doing it.

Thinking all that just makes the tears start back up. I'm so dehydrated, they're just a drizzle, rather than the storm they started off as.

Kenneth hasn't said a word all afternoon, not since Alec explained Danny's plan to him. But, when my chef notices my tears, he comes over and takes my hand. He doesn't say anything, doesn't look at me, just takes my hand and walks next to me, sharing in my grief.

We walk until what I guesstimate is three or four in the afternoon. I don't have a way to judge other than the heat, but it's blazing hot. It's the time of day I'd normally bustle around getting snacks ready and setting up evening events, enjoying the crisp feel of air-conditioning. Today, our dogs are dragging. My feet pine for running shoes. My stomach gurgles and my mouth is as dry as the Dust Bowl. I'm starting to lose focus. Instead of mentally reviewing the items in my boxes that we might use, I keep picturing pitchers full of iced sweet tea, burgers fresh from the grill, a nice soft pillow to sink my head onto.

Alec calls a stop. We don't really halt, so much as just stop dragging our feet. That's how worn down we are.

"We need to rest up," Alec declares. "We're aren't in any shape to do anything like this. Plus, we should wait for darkness. Let's make camp and find something to eat."

Peter Brown and I get assigned to gather mangoes while Kenneth hunts for the more difficult plants he wants to snag for dinner. Alec is going to set up camp.

"It'd be great if you can catch a parrot too," Kenneth calls out after us as we walk off.

I turn around to give him an incredulous stare and Peter just flips him off.

"Well, you don't have to set the bar low," Kenneth grumbles. The sound carries down the hill toward us and Peter and I share a look.

That's all it takes. We double over in laughter. Peter doubles as well as he's able, which isn't much given how swollen he is. I hope to high heaven that my bites don't get that bad.

"Shit, is he for real sometimes?" Peter asks as he holds aside a tree branch for me like a gentlemen. "Catch a parrot. Yeah. Right. I'll just use my bare hands and—" He jumps, whacking a leaf.

"He might just want to complete the flavor profile," I shrug.

That just cracks Peter up all over again. "The flavor profile? We're gonna eat mangoes and fucking leaves over a campfire. In other words—mush. Flavor profile ... Good one," He holds up his hand for a high five.

After I give it to him, I ask. "So, what happened with the gambling?" It is possibly the most direct and uncomfortable question I've asked in my whole life. Usually I hate putting people in the hot seat. But something's tugging at me and I feel like I need to know.

Peter scratches his neck uncomfortably, which just leads to him scratching all over.

"Stop that. You'll start bleeding again. Never mind, you don't needa' answer."

"No ... no. You're right. It's just ... it's fun."

"It's fun?" That can't really be all can it? Losing thirty thousand dollars for fun? I shake my head as I grab a mango that's on the ground and tuck it under my arm.

Peter doesn't answer for awhile. But when he gives me a boost and helps me pluck a second mango stuck on a high tree branch, he confesses, "I've never really thought about it, I guess." He sighs. "I lost my job a few years back. And it was hard. Had to move back home. It used to be something I'd do just to get out of the house, I think. And my first win —it wasn't the lottery—" he gives me a sardonic grin, "but it was enough to get me out of my parent's house. Let me rent a place. And then I kept going. It just kind of snowballed. I didn't even realize it." He shrugs, bending to pick up another fallen mango and groaning as the bend stretches the swollen skin of his back.

I watch him crouch down to scoop up the fruit, wondering about what he said. Is it really possible to just let something like that happen to you? I'd never—but then I think about it. My old job wasn't an addiction. But security was. I used to cling to security like a drunkard clutches the bottle. I didn't used to be much better than Peter Brown.

But I've changed ... I think.

Before coming to this island and meeting my guys, I didn't take risks. Now ... well, I've chosen three guys, and we're stuck in the middle of this chaos. Some risks have been my choice. Some haven't. Either way ... I don't think I'm the same Katie who stepped off that jet a few weeks back. If we get out of this, I don't think there's gonna be any going back to that, which makes me quiet as the possibilities swim through my head.

We spend the next two hours tromping through the forest, getting bit up by mosquitoes who, apparently, think the motherfucking sheer material of my dress is an appetizer. I hit myself so many times to smash the fuckers that I look like a whackadoo, and by the time we tromp back to our campsite with five measly mangoes, I also look like a walking pest-control billboard. Bug bodies and blood drip and ooze off me.

When Kenneth looks up from his pile of leaves and sees what we've got, his expression falls. Like seriously, jaw to the ground, eyes welling up with water, cartoon-level disappointment. "That's it?"

I scratch the back of my neck, "Well, yeah. This island wasn't really designed for people to live off the land."

Kenneth chews his lip in response. His eyes get dark, and I can see all kinds of curse words running over his face—

they're in the microflare of his nostrils, in his furrowed brow, in the tension that pulls up his shoulders.

I cringe, expecting the verbal blows to start.

But he doesn't say anything. He doesn't unleash. He just takes the mangoes from us, and places each one of them in a woven basket along with a handful of nuts and some sticks. Then he shoves them all onto the makeshift prop stick he's turned Alec's hanger weapon into—the bundle of hangers are shoved into the ground and he's bent a couple so that his woven baskets can dangle over the tiny fire he and Alec have made. It's small enough that the smoke won't be a big cloud piercing the canopy of the trees. It should go unnoticed, unless the Russians are tromping through the woods nearby, and then—well, I don't need to think about that part of things.

Kenneth turns to prep some small, round purple fruits he found. He cuts the fruit with his newly acquired pocket knife and hands it around so we can each eat one. Seeing him so upset though, dulls my appetite. I only eat about half my fruit and hand the rest back.

"What are you doing?" Kenneth snaps.

"I'm not hungry."

"You need to eat! Eat!" He thrusts the fruit back in my face aggressively.

I swallow hard and shrink back, grabbing the fruit. I move to the other side of the makeshift camp.

Alec eats his fruit and follows me, while Kenneth pokes a straightened hanger at our measly dinner like he's stabbing it.

"What's his problem?" Alec asks.

I shrug and whisper. "I dunno. He got really mad one time when Heather didn't eat his food. Maybe I offended him?"

Alec shrugs and rolls his eyes. "He's worn out and on edge." His hand comes to rest on my shoulder. "But if he snaps at you again, I'll take care of it."

I lean into him. "Thanks."

"Of course."

"I mean ... for everything." I clarify. "All last night and today."

He leans down and kisses the top of my hair. I'm certain it's a disaster, but he doesn't seem to mind. His hand rubs my upper back, comforting me and reassuring me, but also just surprising me at how comfortable his touch is.

While Kenneth cooks and grumbles behind us, Alec shows me the sleeping area he cleared and the hovel he's made out of brush and a tablecloth we snagged at my villa. I smile at his primitive construction—it's better than I could do, but not by much—thank him, and try to ignore the fact that a ginormous bug just skittered across the tablecloth covering the ground. I'm definitely calling middle at nap time. Even if Kenneth is being a grump, I'd rather he face the bugs than me. Or, maybe I'll just sleep on top of Alec. I imagine his pecs serving as my pillow as we walk back to the fire. Getting swoony is a serious error in judgment on my part. I nearly face plant into the fire. A pair of strong arms saves me, swooping around my middle and pulling me back.

I look up to see the object of my daydream. Night dream? Wet dream? I'm not quite sure. I stare up at Alec's brown eyes and go a little weak at the knees. His gaze is just ... intense, like always.

"You okay?"

"Yeah." I stare up at him sheepishly. At my feet, something starts smoking.

"Out of my way!" Kenneth pushes me aside and reaches his hands for the baskets. One of them is on fire. He yanks it, cursing and shaking his hand like he's gotten burnt. But that doesn't stop him from snatching all of the other baskets out. He lines them up and uses his stolen pocket knife to cut open the baskets. Three of them release the delicious scent of cinnamon and baked almonds. Three of them have gorgeously cooked mangoes that look like pie filling inside. One—well, it's a burnt mess.

Kenneth grits his teeth and hands us the unburnt portions, taking the burnt one for himself.

"You can have mine," I try to push my mango toward him.

"No."

"I don't mind—"

"I do!" Kenneth snaps. He stands and tromps off through the undergrowth, smashing it aside. He's clearly agitated. And I get it. We're all at the end of our ropes—tired, exhausted, and worried. But then he smacks a tree trunk and kicks it. He curses. Alec and I exchange a worried look. Kenneth's mood has been going downhill since the Russians arrived but this ... this is something more than exhaustion.

"Just let him cool down," Peter waves him off as he lifts his woven leaf basket onto his lap and pinches a piece of roasted mango in his fingers. "It'll be fine."

I stare for a second at Heather's former harem contender. Mr. Smooth and Slimy Backdoor. And I ask myself if I want to take life advice from a man who gambled away money he didn't have, planned to pimp that money out of my best friend, and ran away instead of facing his problems. A man who can't even articulate them.

Nope.

I stand up and push my food toward Alec. "You can have extra. I'm gonna talk to Kenneth."

"You sure?"

I put my hand on his shoulder and smile. "Yeah."

Peter makes a scoffing noise as I turn away. "Stupid. Let him cool off."

Alec chucks a pebble at Peter's face. "Shut it."

The part of me that hates confrontation crumples at Peter's words and wants to slink away. But I can't. Kenneth's been getting progressively worse. I don't know if it's sleep deprivation or what, but we all need to be on the same page for tonight. And there are no pools around here I can ask Alec to toss him in so we can hit the reset button. I swallow hard and tromp around a couple bushes, following Kenneth's angry path of destruction pretty easily.

He sits in a small opening in the trees, one that's a perfect circle, with dappled light. But, unlike the meadow for the sparkly vampire I liked to read about before I learned what real romance books were, this opening isn't filled with flowers. It's just bare, like a space one would use to meditate. It has a calming vibe. Kenneth definitely seems to be embracing that vibe, because he's sitting cross-legged, breathing deep, and muttering to himself as he does neck circles.

I sit down next to him, unwilling to interrupt his chi or whatever it's called. I breathe deep and start to mimic him.

After the neck circles, Kenneth opens his eyes. When he spots me, his gaze narrows but he doesn't say anything. He does some back twists. Again, I follow. We go through three or four movements until it seems Kenneth's mood has settled. His eyes no longer have that furious gleam. His shoulders are relaxed.

He stretches out on the ground and stares up at the canopy of the trees. I lay down next to him and just share in the moment, trying to be there, but not overwhelm him if he doesn't want to talk.

After a long stretch of silence, punctuated only by the slap of our hands on motherfucking, buzzard-sized mosquitoes, Kenneth swivels his head to look at me. I turn my head to meet his gaze and give a half smile.

He looks pensive for a moment. But then he says, "I hate being hungry."

That's it. It's all he says before he turns and looks back up at the sky.

I'm confused. That's his big revelation? He acted like he was gonna tell me something significant. Maybe he thought it was significant. He hates being hungry. We all hate it. Does he think he hates it more because he's a chef? Does he mean he gets hangry? That would explain a lot of this afternoon. But I still feel like I'm missing something.

"Why?" I ask.

I almost think he didn't hear me. He takes awhile to answer. But, when he does, he keeps his eyes trained on the leaves above. "My parents went to jail when I was fourteen. Dealers." I turn to look at him, and while his eyes stare straight up, his body tenses. My eyes slide down and see him clenching his fists.

My heart curls up like a fern trying to protect itself. Because I can hear the hurt in his tone. And his pain hurts me. I can just imagine Kenneth, my Kenneth whose smile can light up a room, as an awkward teenager, alone. Abandoned. Just like Heather. I know she used to cry herself to sleep nearly every night those first two years. Not because we've ever talked about it, but because she basically lived at my house. And when she thought all of us were sleeping, she'd shake the bed with sobs. I have no idea if Kenneth had someone to take him in. I have no idea if he had friends or family or anything at all.

"I had to fend for myself," Kenneth adds, his voice soft. "Eventually, I wised up and lied about my age. Got a job at a restaurant. It was the first time in years that I wasn't hungry."

God—I clutch at my chest. Hearing that makes me angry and furious and heartbroken all at once. And now, his single-minded focus on work makes sense. His choice of work. I want to hug Kenneth. I want to wrap myself around him and make all kinds of ridiculous declarations about how I'll take care of him and stick by him and even if he wants to stop the sex, I'll be his friend. Forever. Because if I can put up with Hurricane Heather as a best friend, he'd damn well better believe I can put up with just about anything else.

But I don't do any of that. I don't say any of that. I just lay next to him and accept him. As is. Because sometimes telling the truth is hard enough. The pity that comes with it can be unbearable.

CHAPTER SIXTEEN

HEATHER

So I'm supposed to keep these bozos occupied for hours. But Suity and Blob make that near impossible. Both end up coming within ten minutes of starting to play with themselves, on several different occasions. It doesn't seem to matter if I toss on penis pumps or cock rings. It doesn't matter if I have them butt fuck my Eiffel Tower dildo while I do a little strip show. That shit would give most guys pause, but it's like their dicks are auto-programmed by a microwave timer. Three minutes. Done! *Ding!*

I don't count their orgasms, but they have serious face-palm numbers. Luckily for me, Blob has a little bit of a delay factor between rounds. Moreso than the others, anyway—I probably only have to distract him half as many times. J2 is hot as hell, and I grew up with a little bit of a Terminator crush, so that part's not bad. I even get him to say "I'll be back," once after he comes. And that revs me the hell up. But seriously? Having guys shoot off before they even take care of me ... that's not sex etiquette. It's fucking rude. It's like these guys have never been to an orgy before. They have no stamina, no self control, have no clue what the fuck edging is, even when I try to get the twins to explain it.

Blob's response to their explanation is, "People do this? The edge?"

What the fucking hell? These Russians could probably drink me under the table. But I could sex them under the table, over the table, on the table. They really need to spend far less time chasing people around with guns and more time having fun. It's solid life advice.

When Blob collapses on the couch holding his floppy tits like he can't breathe, I know I need to find a new distraction technique. There's no way these guys can keep up with me for four more hours. I think for a bit about what I could possibly do that might take some time. I mean, when this was a harem competition, Katie set all kinds of shit up for us. Surely, I can use something—I figure it out. Damn! I'm a genius. I get the twins off real quick to ensure all the guys are chillaxing in a post-orgasm haze so I can implement part one of my brand-new, genius plan.

I say, "I gotta pee." I walk over to my bedroom and grab an outfit off the dresser. I take a quick shower to wash off all the cum on my tits—seriously, I get that guys think that's hot, but the aftermath is fucking annoying. It makes me want to rub come inside their asscrack and say, "Good, now don't move. Let me stare at it. It's dry? Okay, you can go wash it off now." I always fucking miss a spot. Today, I'm sure I miss several, because I'm in a hurry. I've got gunmen to distract, bombs to build, it's a busy day.

I toss on some clothes. Probably more than I've worn since my golf date on that other island. But, this next little bit calls for running shoes. So, I wear a purple golf skirt that matches my peekaboos, a low cut t-shirt that will hope-fully keep eyes off my hands and on my chest, and some badass rainbow-colored New Balance trainers that I bought in Utica Square (aka the fancy mall) back home. I stick with commando because I always go commando and honestly, I only packed underwear for the plane to be polite.

I just smile at the twins when they come to check on me. "Just doing my hair," I bat my eyes and use my pick to give myself a part. When I turn on the blow dryer and start doing a blow out to curl my hair, R&R back off. They've stayed over at my villa before, and they know my hair routine can last a couple hours.

Once they're gone, I set down the blow dryer but leave it running.

I climb into the jacuzzi tub that's been the source of many a fun time and yank at the window next to it. It takes a little shoving, and I crack a frickin nail, but I get the sucker open. And then I squeeze my ass out of the villa and book it.

I run past the windows in the living room, making sure the idiots can see me, because the last thing I want is for them to go back to the kitchen. I want them to know I've run. I want them to chase me. And I want them to catch me.

I hear stomping and shouting behind me, which means they're outside. I don't look back. I push my legs to run faster, because those assholes have longer legs. I'm gonna have to hurry to reach my destination before they get their hands on me.

I see my goal over on the left. I shove off the path and head straight for it through the brush, hoping that the bushes and shit will slow these assholes down a bit.

I head toward a building that we haven't used this entire trip. It's white like the others, but instead of being lined with windows, it's all walls. Only a tiny row of windows peek out at the very top of the building, fifteen feet in the air. It's supposed to be like a game hall with a half basketball court, a couple bowling lanes, a pool table, stuff I'm generally not interested in. But Katie had it converted before we arrived into one of the challenges for the guys, a team-building challenge we haven't gotten to yet. She hired someone to make the entire space an escape room.

I slow down, even though I hear the cursing mobsters getting closer. I never really asked Katie about all the details of this sucker. I've never done an escape room before. Now, I'm regretting my ignorance, because I'm gonna have to figure out what the hell I can do here. I know they lock you inside for an hour and you have to solve puzzles or something ... but where's the timer? Do I have to lock the guys in from the outside? Is the timer like a manual thing or like automatic? Do I need a key? Anxiety is an emotion I tend to try to avoid, kinda like I used to try to avoid Dane and his stories about his dachshunds in our old neighborhood. But, here it is, anxiety's knocking at my knees. Fuck. I try to shake it off and hurry the hell up.

I approach the door of the building. It looks like it's a bit more solid than the ones in our villas. It's metal, so at least they can't kick it in so easily. And bingo! A grin crosses my face. Katie made things easy. Or her people did. On the outside of the metal door is a huge digital countdown clock.

The blinking red numbers show one hour on the clock. I pull the handle to test it. It turns easily enough and I pull it open. The room inside is pitch black—I guess Katie must have had the windows blacked out or something to up the creep factor. I don't search for a light switch because I don't give a shit about that. If those bozos get trapped in the dark, all the better for me. I just pull the door wider to try to see if the inside handle turns or if it automatically locks, but the inside of the door has no handle. Score! So, hopefully that means once the door shuts, it's locked and the timer will start.

I test it, letting the door slam shut. Sure enough, the seconds on the clock start ticking down. Awesome.

Behind me, the footsteps get heavier. I look over and J2 is bursting through the trees with his gun out, looking just as scary as Arnold did when his face was all red-laser-eyed robot. My heart starts ticking faster than the countdown clock. Crap. I need to hurry it up.

I feel around the sides of the clock, looking for any kind of adjustment buttons. The first one turns the numbers from red to green. Fuck you clockmaker! That's a waste of a button. I slide my fingers further. The next one does change the time on the screen. But it's the fucking minute hand. It only changes the time to 1:03 after a couple jabs. I glance back. J2 is only steps away. Everyone else isn't far behind him.

My hand slips off the next button. Stupid nerves. I fumble around and find it again. I press quickly, just as J2's hand lands on my shoulder. The time cycles to two and then three before he yanks my shoulder back.

I hear Reval or Rubin behind me shout, "Heather you are in big trouble."

J2 seems to agree, based on the way he's pressing his gun into my back. Sweat trickles down my spine and the feel of that gun. This time, I'm far more worried about it. Suity might not be so dark. But I don't think J2 has any problems with shooting people.

"This was bad move," Suity growls as he gets close.

J2 tries to yank me off the door completely, but I cling to it like a tick on a dog. I have to get them inside. I have to! Fuck! I need a plan! But Katie's the planner—Katie!

"Katie!" I scream, turning my head into the black abyss beyond the doorway. "Run!"

Rubin, Reval, and Blob reach us, but I ignore them, fighting to hold onto the door and clutching the handle as J2 tries to scoop me up by the waist one-handed and pull me away from it. "Katie!" I scream again. "They have guns!"

"Katie? She's here?" One of the twins asks hesitantly.

"No one is here," J2 dismisses him.

R&R disagree. "We should go look. To be sure, no?"

J2's nostrils flare and he grabs me around the waist, yanking me for once and all off the door. He hefts me over his shoulder like a sack of potatoes and holds the door open so his comrades can traipse inside.

As they enter, the lights automatically go on. I can't see inside because of the angle J2 has me dangling at, right near his asshole, but I can see the hospital-like bright lighting. Dammit. That won't make the search take very long. Hopefully, the room isn't easy to see into with a single glance. Hopefully, they have to step inside to look around.

Thankfully, they all go inside and J2 follows.

The chatter starts up in Russian again. And I assume the twins are explaining who Katie is, because I hear her name a couple times.

J2 stays in the doorway and keeps me in his arms. But the door doesn't shut behind us. A sliver of sunlight trails along the ground and up J2's pant leg. Fuck!

I start to wiggle in his arms, and he has to tuck his gun into his waistband to get both hands on me. I lean back and head butt him in the face.

He drops me.

"Ow!" I clutch my forehead.

"Oi!" he exclaims.

I might have just slammed my head into a brick wall. Or maybe an ax. Is his head pointed? It feels like my skull is split open. Damn. I stumble toward the door, grab the edge, and pull it shut just as J2's arms whip me back around.

I grab my aching head and squint at the bright room. Whoa. For a second, I think I might be seeing things. It looks like we might have just stepped into a spaceship. The wall panels are all hexagons. White and silver colors dominate. There are little strips of neon colored lights running floor-to ceiling. There are tiny hallways running like spokes off this main room. And in the center of the room, there's a giant tube that looks like a neon light bulb.

"What the fuck you think?" J2 grabs my neck. Guess he's

not as awed by the room's appearance as I am. He lifts me by my throat and my feet kick a little once I can't touch the ground. He smacks me across the face, hard.

I see red. Literally. My vision blinks red, then black and white, then back to color.

Suity becomes my temporary hero when he says, "Put down her." But, then he becomes an asshole again with his next words. "She must sign over monies still."

J2 drops me and I fall to my knees, coughing and sputtering. "That's right asshole. I'm worth over a hundred mil. Kill me and I'm certain your boss will have no problem wiping your brains off the floor. Of course, there won't be much to wipe!" I ignore the fact that my voice is a hollow wheeze, which is about as threatening as a liver-spotted ninety-year old on oxygen pumping her fist from her wheelchair.

I feel something wet against my thigh and I hear little hiss. I jump. Just behind me at floor level, a fog machines starts up. The floor of the room is slowly covered in fog. The lights on the wall start flashing in a pattern. Red. Red. Green. Blue. A screen projection pops up on the far wall and a grey alien with three antennae starts talking, too low for me to hear. I'm kind of sorry that we never got around to playing this game. Under normal circumstances, this looks like it would be a hell of a lotta fun.

Rubin and Reval are busy searching the little archways, going down the hallways, opening stand-up cabinet doors, looking for Katie.

"She is not in here." Rubin turns to me with his hands on his hips. "Why did you say she is in here, when she is not?"

"She trap us!" J2 gestures toward the door.

All of them turn to look at it. Their eyes scan down and I can tell the moment they realize it doesn't have an interior handle. The temperature in the room shoots up a hundred degrees.

I scrounge up some tears, the kind I'd use on Shane Paul whenever that fucktard was thinking about going on yet another "extended business trip." Tears only worked on Shane Paul about half the time, so my best guess is that I got a 50-50 shot with these guys. Maybe less since they're so pissed. But it's worth a try. I let my lower lip tremble. "Those guys deserve a chance to get away."

Both Suity and J2 start cussing.

"Crazy," Blob grumbles.

Suity pushes past me and tries to open the door even without a handle. He shoves at it. When it won't budge, he kicks it, like a toddler throwing a fit. The only good that does is give him a bruised fucking toe.

I try not to look smug as he howls and clutches his foot. J2 slips past him and starts yanking at the edges of the door as though he can do better. There are no hinges on this side of the door for him to grab onto. It's completely flat. His attempt is completely pathetic. I roll my eyes.

Rubin and Reval come forward. Unlike the others, they don't seem pissed. They seem sad.

"Heather, you don't trust us?"

I'm taken aback, the wind is knocked out of me. They

fucking thought I still trusted them? "What kind of question is that?" I scoff.

They're acting like they're all hurt that I tricked them when they double-crossed me first. Wow. Fucking entitled. And it's like someone's thrown a match on me, and I've just been waiting for the chance to go up in flames. I don't give a shit that we're locked in a fucking escape room and they all have weapons! They want to kill me? I think, *Go ahead. Enjoy stepping around my dead body for the next three hours, you dumb fucks. I hope I death shit on your shoes.*

"You!" I growl, taking a step forward. "You think I would ever motherfucking trust you?" I toss my head back and laugh. I point at J2 and Suity. "At least they don't lie and pretend this could all motherfucking work out. They know they're gonna kill me eventually. I know it. So, fuck you. I'm trying to give the others a goddamned chance."

I shove Rubin and stomp over to the other side of the room, where a clear box full of rainbow-colored crystals sits. I throw the box across the room and scream. Not one of them moves to stop me. They all just stand silently, watching. Because there's nothing else for them to say. Everyone in this room knows that I'm on as much of a countdown clock as that door.

Question is, can I escape before time's up?

"We better get back," Kenneth starts to sit up.

I follow, but his stomach growls.

Dammit. Now that I know what it means for him to be hungry, I wish I hadn't offered Alec my food. I glance around and realize that wherever we've run off to—this little meadow in the woods—it's near the golf course. Danny's villa isn't far.

I grab Kenneth's hand. His eyes avoid mine. Until I yank him sideways and start walking away from our campsite and toward the golf course, forcing him to follow like a lost little puppy.

"What are you doing?" he asks.

"Getting you something to eat."

We skirt the golf course and stick to the tree line so we won't be seen. We move quietly. Neither of us are great shakes at keeping silent, so slow and steady is the best bet. My ears are alert the entire time, listening for voices, for footsteps, for gunshots. But all I hear is the breeze and the stupid squawk of a parrot nearby.

"Cum on my tits!" it screeches. "Motherfucker, cum on my tits!"

I have to bite back a laugh. I'm pretty sure that bird didn't know the phrase before Heather came to this island. It's fucking ironic that she's said that line enough for a parrot to memorize it, since I know she's always complaining about that. My thoughts fly to her, wondering where she's at and what she's doing, hoping she's safe. I feel a tug toward her villa, and part of me wants to tromp down there right away just to get my eyes on her. But Alec is right. We're in no state fit to attack and survive. And we need to make Danny's sacrifice ... I grit my teeth and shove my thoughts in a different direction. No fucking way can I think about that without getting madder than a puffed toad.

I force myself to focus on snacks. I don't know exactly where they're hidden right now, so we're gonna have to search and hope those Russian motherfuckers didn't find them. I yank Kenneth toward Danny's villa, noting the front door is bent but not broken. I try the handle. Unfortunately, it's still locked. I pull Kenneth around the backside, away from the path.

"What are you doing?" Kenneth asks. "There's nothing but a couple candies and bottled water in these villas." He sighs. "If we could go to my kitchen—"

I shake my head. "Too central. They're probably all right around there. And maybe what you said about no food is true in most the villas. But this happens to be Danny's. And that motherfucker is a snack hoarder."

Conveniently, the floor to ceiling living room windows for Danny's villa have been smashed in, just like mine. We step carefully around all the glass, and I make my way to Danny's bedroom. I throw aside the sheets. Nothing. I crouch down on the carpet and look under the bed.

"What are you doing?"

"Assmonkey likes to hide the snacks from me."

"Snacks?"

"Yeah, Alec would bring in chips and stuff. We kinda had an ongoing war—" I say as I yank open the closet doors.

"You don't like my food?" Kenneth voice is quiet. The question is almost a whisper.

I turn around slowly. Crap! "That's not it!" Oh, he's gotta be madder than the snake that married a garden hose. Or worse—hurt. I know how Kenneth feels about his food. Fuck! I don't want him to be hurt. I swallow and carefully think through my next words before I say them. "You're an amazing chef. Your food is orgasmic. Literally. Sometimes though ... I just want chips at midnight."

He closes his eyes and shakes his head.

I'm on pins and needles, waiting for him to say something. I'm about to throw my arms around his waist and beg his forgiveness and swear off junk food for life when he says, "I guess ... I understand. You don't have the same issues with junk food that I do."

I move forward so I can take his hand and stare up at his face. "What?"

He shrugs. "When money was tight, that's what I ate. I'd

figure out what had the most calories and just ... that was it for the day."

My heart sinks. "And now you hate it."

He bites his lip. "It brings back bad memories."

"Well, shit."

He shrugs. "It's better than being hungry. But ... um, I think I want to take a shower real quick if you don't mind."

I nod. I can't tell if he's just trying to get away from me or if he really does hate the gross, sweaty mess that this overnight hike has made us. But all I can do is respect his wishes.

When he leaves, I go back to searching. I find the duffel bag up high behind the fru-fru curtains, balanced on the curtain rod and leaning on the wall. I have no idea how Danny managed to get it to balance up there, but he did. I drag a chair over and yank the bag down, nearly falling backward over the chair in the process.

I unzip the bag. And to me, it's like looking down on a little slice of processed heaven. There are ranch Doritos, Cracker Jacks, Skittles, Starburst—I don't wait, I bust one of those puppies open and go right for the orange—and all kinds of other yummys.

As I chew, I stare at the bag for a minute, not really sure what to do. But Kenneth *has* to eat. We came all this way, and he's too run down. He's gotta be ready to fight. I just need to pull him out of this funk. I rip open a bag of Cheetos as I think. I stick one in my mouth.

An idea comes to me. And almost as soon as it comes, it makes me feel as self-conscious as that girl at the middle school dance who sees her crush leaning against the wall chatting. She eyes him, thinking "this is it, this is my chance," but then when she trots over to him, she gets as tongue-tied and awkward as a newborn calf.

My hands start to shake. But Kenneth needs to eat. Like, life and death needs to eat. He associates this food with awful memories. But other food ... he associates with sensuality.

Maybe I can help him redefine these things he hates. Or maybe this is a terrible idea. Maybe I should just let him go to sleep. Maybe I should just give him a bottle of water and let them nap it off and hope for the best. I don't want to have him get pissed off at me. For some reason, Alec's face pops into my brain like a little fucking annoying Jiminy Cricket. He whispers into my ear, *What do you really think Katie? Do you really think he's gonna get mad at you?*

I go over to Danny's duffel bag. I shuffle through the contents, looking for something that might work. My cheeks burn as if I've already gone over to Kenneth and been rejected and humiliated.

I head out to the living room, to the sink by the bar. I turn on the tap. I gulp down some water and then I undress and use the little towel from the bar-top to wipe myself down. I don't want to interrupt Kenneth's shower. And I won't have the courage to try this if he's already watching.

Once I'm clean, I head back to the bedroom. I grab the black duffel bag. And I make my way to the bed.

THE SHOWER SHUTS off and through the open

doorway to the bathroom, I can see Kenneth rubbing himself down with a towel, facing away from me.

I'm splayed out on Danny's bed, nude, covered in candy and chips. I've painted lines of Cheeto cheese up my neck and on the insides of my thighs which are spread wide, knees out, so that he can look at my core. A line of M&Ms trail up my stomach like buttons. I used caramel corn to make a "bra." There's a little rainbow of skittles above my pot of gold. I'd done that first, thinking I'd open with the cheesy line, "Want to taste *my* rainbow?"

He turns. My heart pounds. Anxiety digs into me like an icepick. And suddenly I'm second-guessing myself. This is a terrible idea. How stupid am I, thinking that I could somehow reprogram his mind? I can't believe I thought of something this dumb. He doesn't have to eat candy or chips.

I should have gone out and gotten more mangoes. I start to sit up, my hands flying into the piles of Doritos, Lays, and other chips that are scattered across the comforter like rose petals. Fuck me! Moving isn't easy. My hands lands on a jagged piece of chip and I yelp, popping up hard and fast. Another shard digs into my ass and I leap onto my knees on the mattress. Candy falls off me like rain. The caramel corn does not. The damned Caribbean humidity has melted some of the caramel. The popcorn sticks to my breasts like little tumors.

"Katie!" Kenneth rushes into the room. He stops stock still at the sight of me.

I try to scramble off the bed, but it's like I've built my own torture device. I'm getting stabbed from every direction.

"What are you doing?" Kenneth puts his hands up and

approaches me cautiously, eyeing me up and down and then looking around the room.

Shame coats me like hot grease. My skin burns. Insecurity heats my insides and runs down my cheeks in molten tears. God I'm such an idiot. Kenneth takes a step closer. He sees the bumps all over me and jumps back. "God! Did something attack you? Are there hornet stings ..."

I looked down and I realize he can't tell what's all over me in the shadows because the curtains are closed and I left the lights off. All he can see is my body covered in bumps.

I swipe at my stupid tears. "I'm fine. I'm fine. It's just candy. And caramel corn. Maybe some chips."

"What?"

I bite my lip as I fumble for words. "You're hungry. You said eating these things reminded you of back then. I was just trying to ... give you a different sort of perspective. You know, since sexy times and food seem to be your thing. But then I decided that was a terrible idea. And I tried to get up. And that was a mistake. Because I now think I hate Frito-Lay's as much as you do. I'm pretty sure there are about fifty broken, pointy pieces of them digging into my ass right now." Once I start confessing it all just pours out. My filter evaporates.

Kenneth closes the distance between us. He raises his hand my face and swipes away one stray tear. He gives me a soft smile. "It's really sweet, what you were trying to do."

"No, it's stupid," I sniffle.

"Not many women embrace my kink. Looks like you were willing to go all out."

"I just made a fool of myself, is all."

"Isn't that what you're supposed to do? When you like someone?"

My insides go from humiliated to humming. "I dunno."

"I do. Thank you, Katie." He leans down and gently kisses my lips. At first, the kiss is a chaste gentle sweep over my lips. Just a way for him to erase my embarrassment. But something about the fact that he didn't laugh at me and that he thought I was thoughtful, makes me lift up on my toes and push harder against his lips. My teeth sneak out and bite his lower lip.

He groans. "You're sweet and a kinky freak. I love it."

Kenneth pulls me closer and his hands trace the undersides of my breasts as our tongues battle. I forget all about everything that happened before when the pads of his thumbs gently rub the tips of my nipples. I press into them, wanting more than just a tease, wanting him to pinch and pull on my nipples, but he moves his hand back, only keeping the gentlest contact. I whine into his mouth. He breaks our kiss and bends quickly; his lips clamp down on my nipple. He sucks hard and my exhale becomes a moan of pleasure.

My hands reach out and dig into Kenneth's biceps. I slide my hands around back toward his triceps, which are a nice, thick, hard band of muscle. I trace up to his shoulders and along cords of his neck. My hands settle in his hair just as he moves to my other breast. He chuckles and eats off all the caramel corn pieces stuck to it. And then he treats that nipple just like the first.

My body starts to shiver with anticipation as he slides his

hand down my stomach, slowly tracing a twisting path toward my core. He's such a fucking tease. I think Kenneth must love appetizers just as much as dessert. But I'm not a patient woman. I arch forward, pushing my pussy toward his hand. He parts his index and middle fingers so that they don't touch my nub. He uses them to stroke the sides of my lips.

His mouth releases my breast and he slides his nose along my clavicle, whispering, "Do you want it Katie? Tell me how bad you want it."

His tongue starts to trace up my neck but he pauses when he reaches the Cheeto powder. He pulls back and chuckles, then playfully nips my neck."You thought you'd tempt me with Cheeto cheese?"

"Well, it is a gateway snack food," I reply. "No one can resist licking Cheeto cheese."

He proves me right. He leans back down and traces over each side of my neck with his tongue, pointing it and flattening it, then swirling it, making sure he's gotten up every last bit of cheese. By the time he's done, I'm a panting mess. He could fuck me right now, no further prep needed. I'm slicker than an umbrella in a rainstorm.

I yank on his hair and pull him back up to kiss me. I crush my lips to his and then whisper, "I need you, Kenneth. I need you to fuck me. Hard."

He instantly responds, moving his hand from my neck to the back of my head. He yanks my hair back and then bends over me, nipping at my neck. Then he crushes me into him —until a chip fragment still stuck to my stomach stabs us both.

He breaks our kiss. "Ow! What the hell is that?

"A chip."

He laughs, and to my surprise, he squats down and sucks the chip fragment into his mouth. He crunches it between his teeth and then licks and nips at my stomach. He moves on to another fragment on the underside of my breast and does the same. This time when he licks, I can't help the soft shiver that goes up my spine. Fuck. I need him. Now. I push his head down, but he just leans back and smiles at me.

"It's so cute to see you think you're in charge."

"Kenneth!" I plead.

"No. You're a bad girl." He smacks my ass. "When I walked in here, I thought you'd been attacked by hornets or something. I thought you were going into anaphylactic shock. You had bumps everywhere."

He smacks my ass again. "You should have stayed on the bed and let me see you like that."

I laugh nervously. "I had my legs spread for you. I had a whole rainbow made of skittles, and I was gonna ask ..."

I trail off as Kenneth groans and puts his mouth where I want it. He points his tongue and slides it up and down my opening, not pushing inside, just teasing my nerve endings until my mind fritzes like TV static.

"Your rainbow is magically delicious," Kenneth leans back and grins.

My face glows redder than Rudolph's. "Don't say that! God, I'm so dumb. I'm just gonna go crawl into a hole and die now."

Kenneth laughs. "Oh no. I'm the one who's gonna crawl into a hole. Your hole." He pinches my nipple as he says it.

If it's possible to be turned on and comically relieved at the same time, that's what I am. I laugh hard.

When I'm finally able to meet his eyes, I whisper, "I just wanted to make you feel better."

His responding grin is one I haven't seen before. It's not playful Kenneth, not seductive Kenneth. It's tender. "You did. Now, I'm forever going to associate Rolo's with the brown spots all over your ass."

"No!" I turn and check my butt. There's a few crumbs on it, but there are no brown marks. I was careful about the chocolate placement—thank goodness. Because otherwise, chocolate might always remind me of humiliation and shit stains. It should never be ruined like that.

Kenneth's hand trails over my abdomen, knocking off the few crumbs that are still clinging to me as he stands back up. His mouth brushes against mine. It's a soft kiss, but he quickly turns it into more. He thrusts his tongue inside my mouth and I respond by kissing him back with abandon. The heat builds as his mouth dominates mine, his tongue swirling around mine, his lips sucking my tongue into his mouth. Kenneth is demanding. His hands wander down and clutch my hips, squeezing hard. I press my naked body against his, crumbs be damned. But I guess Kenneth doesn't have the same outlook on crumbs. Because he backs his body away and chuckles. "You are quite the dirty girl, Katie. I think we need to clean you up."

I bite my lip, suddenly self-conscious, suddenly concerned

about the time, when two seconds ago I didn't give a good goddamn. "Maybe we should get back to the others."

Kenneth eyes sparkle as he stares down at me. "You said you wanted to take care of me. That you wanted to feed me." His fingers drift down my stomach and he drags his index finger over my slit. He dips his finger inside me and strokes a few times. Then he slides his slick finger out of me and pulls it up to his mouth, licking it clean. "Come on, Katie. I need to eat." With that, Kenneth takes my hand and walks me to the shower.

He gets the water warm enough to be comfortable, but cold enough that when he pulls the shower head off the wall and runs the spray along my body, my nipples still pebble.

"Oh," I gasp, grabbing onto his shoulders.

"Oh no, dirty little Katie. You need to put your hands here." He wraps his fingers around my wrists and places my hands on the tile wall behind me. "When I feed, I don't like to be distracted. I don't like interruptions. I like to eat in total silence so I can appreciate all the flavors."

Oh my fucking hell, his words alone have just caused my pussy to spasm. My knees bend a little as my insides contract. I don't know if mental orgasms are possible, but if they are I fucking just had one. Shit. Dominant Kenneth is fucking hot. I keep my hands on the wall of the shower as he trails his mouth down my breasts. He laps at my left nipple, using the hand-held sprayer to stimulate the other. My nipples are normally sensitive, but when I'm getting a hot, warm mouth on one and a cool jet of water on the other at the same time—my body doesn't know what to do with itself. Everything in me just tightens.

"No moving, Katie," Kenneth pops off my nipple and rasps before he sticks the sprayer onto my pussy.

Fuck! It's freezing! At least that's what my pussy thinks. And I want to crawl up the wall tiles and escape, only Kenneth grabs onto my wrists and holds me still. Even so, I start to shake. My libido starts to ebb. If my kitty could hiss, she'd be doing it.

Seconds later, Kenneth drops the sprayer, kneels, and presses his hot mouth to my slit. He exhales, and the chill I felt turns into a hot, humid mist. He noses my slit, exhaling up and down the length of it, warming it all the way back up. My hips tilt of their own volition, seeking his mouth. But he puts his hands on my hips to steady them. "I'm about to eat, Katie. Don't move, or I might lose my appetite."

I tense my legs, trying to hold perfectly still as his fingers part my folds and his hot tongue slides up my center. Fuck! The tease makes me want to shiver. I feel like a soda can that's been shaken and dropped. The pressure bubbles up. I'm so close to spilling over the edge, to exploding. A little whimper escapes.

Kenneth smacks the inside of my thigh and detaches himself. "That's your warning. Next time, I'm spanking this hot cunt."

Dammit! His dirty talk is just as yummy as his dirty mouth. And the very second his tongue reconnects, I shatter. My body becomes a living, fizzling pop rock. I love bossy Kenneth. Bossy Kenneth doesn't stop eating me out, not until his tongue has plunged inside and he's stirred me up with his fingers and brought me to another climax. This time, I can't stop the bucking. My hands can't help themselves. I reach out and grab Kenneth's dark hair and buck wildly into his face, throwing my head back and screaming.

He draws it out, his tongue going in figure eights to keep bumping over my sensitive clit every so often. When I finally can't take anymore, I shove his head away.

He just grins and wipes his mouth with the back of his fore-arm. "Well, I hope those assholes with guns didn't hear you."

My hand slaps over my mouth and my eyes go wide. "I'm sorry. I didn't—"

Kenneth just grins. He stands and spins me around so that I'm facing the shower wall. "If I'm gonna die, at least let me die happy."

He pushes lightly on my back and I bend. It's seconds before I think to ask, "Condom?"

I turn back to see him rolling one on.

"He had some in the bathroom drawers." Kenneth spits on the condom to lube it up and I can't help but notice how thin his dick stretches the condom—his dick is so thick—before he turns my head back around. Then he slides into me. I groan because he feels so good as he pushes past my still-sensitive folds.

"Fuck, yes. Now I don't give a shit if they come." Kenneth says. He pumps into me slowly, grabbing onto my hips and pushing my back down further, so my ass is lifted toward him. "Katie, mmm. Yes."

He alternates between pumping hard and fast and slowing down to a leisurely pace whenever he gets too close to finishing. Eventually, he uses his feet to make me spread mine, widening my stance and leaving me open and vulnerable. His hands reach around me to rub my clit in slow, maddening circles. Even when he pumps fast and hard, he doesn't go faster on my clit. Kenneth keeps me wound tight, on edge, begging him. I think he loves to hear me say please.

I fucking love to say it. No guy has ever dragged things out for me the way he does. No one has ever made sex a full-on out-of-body, out-of-my-mind experience like Kenneth. So I don't just endure his teasing, I embrace it, as my pussy heats up and tingles in ways I didn't even know were possible.

Finally, Kenneth shoves me up against the shower wall, so that my face is turned sideways and my nipples are pressed tight against the cold tiles. He fucks me hard and fast, and his fingers start furiously circling my clit.

"Come, Katie. Come now!" he commands.

And I do. My mind is full of hot wet sparkles, molten chocolate, fluffy clouds—full of complete and utter mindless, discombobulated bliss.

Kenneth comes a few pumps later with a groan. He shoves his body up against mine and leaves himself sheathed for a minute or two after. I can feel him flexing his dick inside me as it softens, drawing out his own pleasure just a few more seconds.

Finally, Kenneth steps back. He turns the water off and holds out a hand to me. He helps me out of the shower, disposes of the condom, and then proceeds to towel me off. He won't let me do it myself. I just smile as he dabs at the water droplets on my skin as if I were a porcelain doll. The contrast is so funny, when he was just shoving me around moments before. Once I'm dry, he dries himself and we head into Danny's room.

Kenneth eyes the mess on the bed, then plops down on the edge of it and grabs a ranch-flavored Dorito.

"Still can't believe you did this."

I blush and give a one-shoulder shrug.

"You must like me."

A fire erupts right on my face.

Kenneth just laughs. "Good thing I like you too, Moon Pie."

"What?"

"You'd rather be Sweet Tart? Or Ruffles? I kinda like that one, too. Cause you're easy to ruffle."

I come forward and smack him on the shoulder. "You're not naming me after a snack food."

Kenneth leans up and gives me a peck on the lips. I can taste the ranch Doritos after his kiss. He just sits back and smirks. "Hell yes, I am."

And his smack on my ass settles the matter.

CHAPTER EIGHTEEN

HEATHER

The Russians start chatting again in gobble-d-gook and I try to ignore them as I sink down to sit in the opening of one of the hallways off the main room. This particular hallway has a number of windows enclosed in glass with a bunch of weird-shaped gadgets inside. They might be futuristic ray guns or dildos, I don't know.

Those arctic monkeys pretend I don't exist; I pretend they don't exist; and we're all fucking happy for twenty minutes, until they figure out what the fuck the escape room is all about.

They start pressing buttons, which light up and make musical sounds like a piano.

I cross my fingers and hope that the song they have to figure out and play is some all-American shit that they've never heard of. But damn Katie and her thoughtfulness to my harem's diversity.

The stupid song they have to play in order to beat that puzzle is "Mary Had a Little Lamb."

Fuck! It takes them under five minutes to solve. They whoop like teenage boys who just drilled a spy-hole into the girls' locker room.

When they hit that final note, my chest tightens and I want to punch one of them in the face to loosen it back up. If I get out of here and find that idiot that designed this room, I'm gonna lock them in an escape room of my own and make them have to play the most obscure Phish song ever in order to get the fuck out. Dumbass! How are these puzzles gonna take an hour, much less the three I put on the door, if they're that easy?

I can't let them get out early! I don't know how long it takes to build a bomb. I chew my nails and watch them move onto the next puzzle. They're lining up shapes on some wall-magnet thing.

Crap. These buttheads are good at this. They're gonna get out.

There's only one thing I can do.

Sabotage.

I stand up slowly and start shaking my leg. Then I walk with a little limp.

Rubin or Reval glances over.

"My leg's asleep," I grumble, not quite too him, hoping that he'll buy it.

I walk along the perimeter of the room, looking for a puzzle piece—a magnet—anything small I could steal or break.

My eyes fall on the box of crystals I tossed. The guys opened them up while they were figuring out the Mary Had a Little Lamb puzzle, unsure what they'd need to solve it. The crystals haven't been used yet.

Those crystals have to be important for something. I stand in front of the box and reach down, like I'm rubbing my aching calf muscle. But really, I grab a thin, hexagonal, rainbow crystal and hide it in my hand. It's shaped roughly like a carrot and I briefly wonder if I could use it to stab one of them. It might take out an eyeball, but it's pretty rounded on the end, so I'd have to gouge and dig.

The mental image that brings up makes me wanna puke. Not to mention the fact that it would probably get me shot dead. I think I'll stick with hiding the crystal.

I tuck the crystal into the waistband of my skirt and wander slowly to one of the hallways, sure to keep my arm covering its location. I keep up the sore leg act. But the crystal is kind of awkward, digging into my side as I walk. And if I don't dead-arm, then it's definitely bulky enough to see. I can't just leave it in my skirt.

I press myself back into a dark corner of the hallway. I make sure all those jerkwads are looking away, then I reach my hand into my skirt and grab that crystal. Right about now, I wish I was a panty girl. But even then, the crystal would be too long for them not to notice. It would totally tent my skirt if it moved around.

I have to hide the evidence of my sabotage. I finger the crystal. It's on the thin side. Where to put it... my decision's made for me as J2 comes into the hallway.

"Find anything?" he asks.

"Nope," I squeak, my hands flying behind my back.

He starts examining the symbols that are carved into the walls around us and my hands edge underneath the back of my skirt. I change my position on panties. Now, I'm grateful that I didn't put them on to block my access further. I slowly work the crystal up the back of my skirt in a way that I hope J2 doesn't notice.

I'm sweating, my breath is shallow, but I'm trying not to let it get loud as my eyes are glued to J2, freaked that he might figure out that I'm up to something.

As his eyes swivel to mine, his brow scrunches. "What you doing?"

"Nothing!" My answer comes out too fast and squeaky, almost like it's Katie talking.

J2 stomps over to me and my hands are fumbling, shaking, shoving at the crystal. Finally, I find an opening and shove. And that crystal is slurped right up inside my ass.

J2 leans over me and yanks my hands out from behind my back. Luckily, they're empty. "What you try to hide?" He grips my jaw.

Just then, the crystal starts to slip. Fuck! I clench my ass. I absolutely cannot have that fucker fall out right now. Fuck! Fuck! Why is it thinner than your average butt plug? I'm totally gonna ream Katie about her crystal selection. She should have known I'd get my freak on in the escape room.

J2 stares at me, awaiting an answer.

"I kinda have to pee," I mutter the first thing that comes to mind. "And we're stuck in here. So I thought I'd try to come back here in the corner."

J2 drops my jaw, shakes his head, and stomps off in disgust.

I let out a huge breath. Crisis averted. Now I just have to keep this thin little crystal up my ass for the next few hours.

It slips again and my hands slide back to cover my butt.

Goddammit.

That might be easier said than done.

CHAPTER NINETEEN

KATIE

After Kenneth's eaten three or four of the Snickers from the chocolates I left in Danny's duffel, we change into fresh clothes.

As I slip on one of Danny's golf shirts instead of that smelly, slutty dress, my throat clenches. He better make it. I can't even—I force myself to keep moving, pulling on some of his athletic shorts and pulling the drawstring tight. The shorts are basically capris on me. But they have pockets. And I'm gonna need pockets for our plan.

I take a quick inhale of Danny's fresh laundry scent and tell the universe that she'd better send him back to me. Or else. I smooth down the green striped shirt, glad that Danny's always worn fitted shirts. Even so, I still look like I'm running around in a bag, but at least it's not so loose that I'm worried about it flying up in my face.

Kenneth changes into some of Danny's tennis clothes, grabs changes for the other guys, including some sandals for Alec, and then grabs the duffel with the remaining candy bars. He tosses the clothes inside and we head out.

Peter Brown is sitting at camp, scratching himself, when we get back. Alec's nowhere to be found.

"Where's Alec?" I ask the obvious question as Kenneth tosses some clothes and food to Peter.

Peter digs into a Snickers bar before he answers. "Mmm. Looking for you."

I sigh. Dammit. The sun's about to set and the last thing we need is to be separated. Shit. This is my fault. I should have come back and told him we were leaving before just dragging Kenneth off. But all I thought about was getting Kenneth fed.

I'm about to run randomly through the trees when I turn and see Alec behind me, glaring down at me.

"I'm sorry," I whisper.

He just nods and I want to curl up in a ball and hide from his disapproval.

But then he comes forward and crushes me into a hug. And that hug says a thousand things. It says he was fucking worried. He was scared. He's relieved. He cares. I stroke his back, trying to reassure him.

Eventually, he lets go and steps back. "Just tell me so I don't think you've been taken next time."

I nod.

When he releases me, Kenneth tosses the duffel bag at him

and says, "She took me over to Danny's stash for food. It's better than burnt mangoes."

"Why the hell aren't we waiting over there?" Peter Brown complains.

Kenneth raises a brow. "You think the Russians are more likely to do another round of searches there? Or drag their butts through the forest—which, I might point out, they've avoided so far?"

That shuts Peter up. So does the candy bar I lob at him.

Alec digs into the bag and his expression when he eats his first candy bar is nothing short of blissful.

He and Peter eat their fill of candy and drink bottled water we took from Danny's villa. They change—Alec groans in relief when he pulls off the suit and gets to toss on sandals, even if his toes protrude a little over the edge. Danny's shirts are way too tight for Peter Brown's swollen body, the shirt keeps rolling up his swollen abdomen, so eventually he gives up and throws his shirt down, opting to face the mosquitoes for another night. It's his funeral. I shrug as he grabs a walking stick off the ground to help his sore body navigate down the hill, and then we set out for my villa.

I go through the list of items we need to find out loud. With each step we take, my tension grows. It's mid-afternoon. The face off will be soon. We want to hit them once it's dark. This might be my last day ... ever. I blow out a breath. Only, I can't think like that. I need to focus. Plan, like Alec said. I need to get shit done so that everything Danny's done for us ... I need to plan.

We make it to my villa after about half an hour of hiking

and that's when I feel like I can finally breathe, because that's when I can start grabbing things, making things, giving orders, executing plans, preparing instead of worrying. The first hour is spent just digging through my boxes, separating out things into piles of "to use" and "probably not." The first pile keeps growing.

Next, we have a blow circle, which is far less exciting than it sounds. We all sit on the floor of my living room and blow up twenty-five sex dolls. Why? Because Heather's a kinky bitch, I do what she says when she says click "Buy Now," and because we need decoys.

"Stop blowing so hard, your doll's bending mine!" Peter complains to Kenneth.

"From what I hear, you're the expert at blowing," Kenneth quips.

"Fuck you!"

"You would."

The room fills with dolls and it gets fucking crowded. When we've got them done, I hand out strips of twine and everyone ties their dolls into bundles. But—problem. We can't fit the bundles out the door. Peter tries to squeeze five of his dolls through at once and almost pops his Asian dolly against the door frame. She catches on a piece of wood and a loud fart noise fills the room.

"Dammit, Peter, you just made your doll queef," Kenneth shakes his head.

"Fuck you—push them through," Peter says, yanking from the other side of the door. The Asian girl's leg starts to deflate and I rush over. I do emergency surgery with a bit of duct tape. Her leg's a goner. It's now a tiny, floppy bit of plastic. But the rest of her survives. She'll still be a decent target.

I yell to Peter, "They aren't gonna fit, you have too many."

We end up throwing my comforter over the glass shards on the ground and dragging the dolls out through the broken sliding glass door in the living room. We hike out toward our target spot and tie the bitches off to trees.

We reconvene at my place for snacks and water after the airheads have been distributed.

Then we split up to go set up various other parts of the plan.

Alec loads Kenneth up, handing him a gun to tuck into his waistband and then an entire box full of crepe paper roses, paper napkins, paper towels, and electric firelighters. He'll use those as kindling to start fires in the wetter parts of the rain forest that borders the villas. We're gonna try to use smoke and drive the mobsters out to the sports complex that I had commissioned into an escape room; it's the building closest to the runway, and farthest from any other buildings. They won't have a lot of options to hide over there. And if they run inside that building—well, all the better for us, I think smugly.

Kenneth also tucks a giant penis piñata under his arm, a rope dangling from its tip so he can hang it. We've filled it with all the fireworks I could find from a display I'd originally intended to use the final night. It includes some mega-illegal shit. In case the fires don't catch on quickly enough, maybe the burst of sound will at least send the bad guys scurrying in the right direction.

Alec hauls off a load of very realistic, plastic snakes and very real broken glass—courtesy of the hundred pack of glass butt plugs Heather ordered—to drop along some of the side paths. I don't know how great of a deterrent either will be, since the Russians have shoes. But Peter Brown seems freaked by the snakes at least.

"What the fuck are those here for?" he asked when I first opened the box.

"Oh, I was gonna use those for the pits in the obstacle course, but then the trainer guy didn't really like them. Overkill or something."

Since Peter won't carry the box with the snakes, I load him up with the heavier box. It's got several bulk-size jars of oil and body syrup. Heather's fantasy chocolate syrup wrestling contest materials are donated to a higher cause. I cross my fingers that between scary, slimy, sticky, and sharp, we can keep those Russians on the path we want them to take.

While the guys set up items for the path, I set off toward the less inhabited side of the island, toward the escape room where we eventually want everyone to end up. I set up a couple of Super Bowl level confetti cannons first. Then I haul a sack full of LED spotlights on my back, trying to take as many as I can in one trip. And then I painstakingly climb trees and wedge them in. The jerkwads are about as easy to shove in place as a tooth-filling. They don't like to cooperate. But, at least I don't have to worry about cords or this would be impossible. Thank the lucky stars Heather had an unlimited budget and I sprang for the battery-operated kind.

I rub my shoulders as I climb yet another tree, dragging the final spotlight with me. I've put up at least twenty so far. I slide in a red gel over the light on one side and a blue gel on the other. Then I carefully climb back down, which is not frickin' easy in over-sized men's clothing that likes to get caught on every damn twig. I eye the sky as I walk back. The sun's edging closer to the tree line. After that, it will be sunset. Almost time.

When I get back to my villa, I don't see anyone in the living room, but I hear the shower running. I cautiously make my way into my bedroom, heart pounding. I mean, it's unlikely that one of those Russians would come all the way out here to shower. Unless they sent someone to guard their perimeter. But, still, he'd have seen our mess and gone back to report. My brain tries to talk my amped up veins down. Carefully, I peer around the door. The outfit Alec was wearing is on the floor. I put a hand on my heart and try and breathe deep and calm the fuck down.

I call out—so that Alec knows it's me and doesn't burst out with a gun.

"Be right out!" he says.

"Okay!" I call back.

I go double check the other rooms, but Peter and Kenneth aren't anywhere to be found.

I walk back into the bathroom just as Alec is wrapping his towel around his waist. I can smell my body wash on him and I am so grateful I went with tropical coconut and not something super girly like strawberries. No, the smell of coconut just makes me think of tanning and oiling Alec's nicely browned stomach.

I snap my eyes from his stomach to his face, realizing I'm sleep deprived and my thoughts are wandering. I shake my head to clear it and ask the question I came in here to ask. "Wasn't Peter with you?"

He shrugs, sending rivulets of water down his chest. And dammit, my eyes fixate on those drops as they near his nipples. My tongue licks my lips. I'm tired, and fucking amped up after thinking someone else was in here. Somehow that equates to being hyper aware of everything about Alec. Well, that's not quite true. I've always been aware of Alec. From the second I saw him, he drew me in and made my head spin like a hurricane.

Alec lifts the towel to dry his hair, and my eyes snap to his face. He's smiling. He knows what's running through my head right now. I have to work hard, way too hard, to keep my eyes respectfully on his face. His grin only turns into a chuckle as he answers my question about Peter Brown. "Yeah, Pete said he had to shit. I told him to go do it in another villa, since we're stuck here for the next two hours 'til the sun sets."

I make a face. Yeah, definitely don't want to smell whatever turds Peter's been cooking up after two days of eating in the forest. He's probably gotten some kind of virus so it's probably poop soup. "Thanks for that."

"Anytime. Happy to help you out any way I can." Alec lets his tone get suggestive as he turns away and hangs up his towel, giving me yet another opportunity to eye his ass and those hot-as-hell lower back dimples. I just want to dig my fingers into them. My hands even lift a little and I can't even stop them. His body is like the North Pole and I'm just a magnet. I can't control it. My eyes drift down over his muscular calves. Shit, even his legs are hot.

He turns back and smirks, catching me. "Are you checking me out?"

My heart skips and I can hardly believe my own audacity when I say, "Always." But it's true, every single thing about Alec—from his macho persona to his huge muscles to his fearless attitude, even his aggressive life lessons is #*goals*, as the brace faces used to say at work. He's kind of what I wish I could be. Being around him, makes me dazed and brave in the same moment. I feel so lucky to have met him.

Before I realize it, I've moved in front of him. I stand staring up at his gorgeous coffee-colored eyes. I watch a drop of water slide down his nose and land on his chin. I lift my hand and use my thumb to brush aside the droplet. I end up rubbing my hand back and forth along the scruff that's grown since he hasn't been able to shave.

My stomach wobbles as I touch him and I'm not sure why. Maybe because I'm not really sure what I'm doing. I don't really have a plan. Which isn't normal for me. I live for planning, love it. But one look at Alec and I feel like a fairy princess wearing a flower crown in a daydream. Everything becomes unreal. All my real-life, grown-up plans get hazy. Despite my nerves, I keep going. I can't seem to resist. My finger drags across his jawline and then traces the pulse in his throat. It jumps under my touch. And just knowing that I excite him makes me flush with pleasure.

I draw my hand, away but Alec catches my wrist. And he places my hand on his chest, right over his rapidly beating heart. We stay like that, eyes locked, hearts racing, for what feels like minutes, but must only be seconds.

And then, suddenly, Alec's arms are around me and he draws me up against his chest. He grabs onto my legs and wraps them around his waist and he carries me into my bedroom.

He doesn't speak but he goes right for my dresser and grabs a condom. Then he takes me over to my bed and throws me onto the mattress fully clothed.

"Get naked, Alec growls.

My body tightens in anticipation. I try to give Alec a sultry grin as I pull off the golf shirt I've been wearing, but I'm pretty sure I fail miserably. I slip off the shorts and sandals quietly and then sit. He just stares at me, his gaze dark and unyielding, demanding something from me. I'm not sure what. But whatever he wants, I want to give it to him. I swallow hard as I watch him harden just from the strength of our stare. He rolls the condom on but doesn't make another move to pleasure himself.

He orders, "Lay back. And spread your legs. Let me look at you."

I do as he says. I arrange my hair and fan it out above my head. Then I lay flat on my back, palms up. I let my legs fall apart in a wide 'X' so he can see all of me. He watches for a long time. And even though he doesn't command me to stay still like Kenneth did, I can tell he wants me to; I can tell he wants me waiting and anticipating, completely still like a little fuck doll. Goosebumps form on my skin as I have that naughty thought. I imagine him calling me that. My nipples tighten. I imagine him fucking me in front of the guys and calling me that and pleasure starts to heat my sex without him even moving a muscle or saying a word. The anticipation spreads until my entire body thrums.

That's the moment that Alec climbs onto the bed and hovers over me. He lowers himself down slowly, until he's resting on his elbows and the rest of his body warms the length of mine. He rests on top of me for a moment, just skin to skin. And every single one of my synapses shouts for joy. His body is so hot and warm and all encompassing. Every point of connection is magical. My breath quickens. His dick twitches against my stomach. And still he doesn't move, doesn't speak, he just stares deep into my eyes.

It's as if I've been invisible my whole life and someone can finally see me.

A tear forms but I won't let it fall. My eyes just grow glassy.

That's when Alec gently lowers his face and kisses me. Just lips, just the sweetest, most chaste, most tender kiss I've ever experienced. The dam breaks and a tear tracks down my cheek. My mind starts to form thoughts but they all fizzle and fade when he kisses me. Some part of me knows Alec is showing me a new side of himself, a side he doesn't often let out.

When he grips my hair and gently pulls my head back, he stares down at me. He drops his hold on the back of my head and begins tracing my hairline with his hand. "You have goosebumps. Let's get you under the covers."

"But then if Kenneth comes back, he can't see."

Alec gives me a half grin as he rolls over to my side, sits up, and then pulls me up into a seated position next to him. "What makes you think I want Kenneth to see?"

I bite my lip. "But I thought —"

"Katie, you're my more." And then his lips are back on mine. Not gently this time. This time Alec tries to burn the meaning of the word into my brain, into my body, into my soul.

His hands slide down and stroke the sides of my breasts. He lifts me up and sets me on his lap, straddling him. Then he reaches around around me pulls the comforter from the bottom of the bed and wraps it up around my shoulders like a cape. He holds it in place as he trails kisses down my neck. And then he falls backward unexpectedly, bringing me with him. A giggle slips out as I fall on top of him.

He releases the coverlet and lets his hands wander. His grip keeps me secure, my hips aligned with his. His hands move inward and cup my breasts, squeezing and kneading them. His mouth dips down and he sucks a nipple between his lips, his teeth just teasing but not biting the tip.

One of his hands moves to my back and slides down slowly. He traces the crack of my ass and then dips into my folds. He spreads my wetness and then strokes, alternating suction on my nipple and long, slow strokes up my slit.

I moan. I try to hump his hand or rub against his hard shaft, but he stops sucking and simply says, "Wait."

So I just lay there, clawing at his shoulders as he resumes his slow, steady torture of my body. My mind becomes a tangle of wires and I feel like someone ran a semi truck into an electric fence. I'm sizzling, sparking heat and broken thoughts and spinning wheels. Fuck!

My hands reach down and I jerk Alec's face off my chest. I can't wait another damned second. "I need you," I whimper. Because I can't hold all this inside anymore. This electricity needs to arc out. I need to ground myself.

Alec's eyes are hooded. He doesn't respond, but he doesn't protest. So I reach back and throw his arm off me, pulling him out of my core. I lift my hips and sink down on him. That's all it takes. That one singular stroke and I fucking scream.

Alec's smile when I come back down isn't smug or triumphant. It's sweet. He strokes my cheek and gives me another soft kiss.

And then he rolls me over and takes me to that high again.

ONCE WE'RE DRESSED, we head into the living room. "I can't believe they're not back yet," I say. "I was pretty sure by that third orgasm that we were gonna get an audience whether we wanted one or not."

Alec shrugs. "Peter's not looking good. I wouldn't be surprised if he spent this entire time in the bathroom."

I grab my remote controls. I hand one to Alec and pocket the control for the lights. I grab my bullhorn and start playing with the buttons as we wait. I'm feeling antsy.

"Don't you think they should be back by now?" I ask. I

glance outside through the shattered living room window. The sun is hovering just above waterline. It'll be dark soon.

Alec goes to the door and checks outside. "Yeah, it couldn't hurt. I don't know which villa Peter took off to, but we know the route Kenneth was gonna go."

I stand up, glad to be doing something other than sitting. "Am I a bad person if I say I don't really care about Peter?"

Alec checks the magazine on his weapon and then carries it at his side as we leave. "Nah. I'd say you're normal."

I gulp. "Normal? Dating three guys?"

"Okay. Extraordinary. Sorry. I'm not so good at the supportive shit."

I laugh as we enter the trees. "But are you still okay with it all? I mean, after what just happened?" I hope he's okay. I just don't want to hurt him. Because Kenneth and Danny— my heart gives a painful little tug—are just as important.

"We're a team, Katie." And then Alec takes the lead, as if that one sentence settles the matter.

Which, I hope it does. I really, really hope. Just about as much as I really hope that this pie-in-the-sky, smoke-and-mirrors plan works.

After fifteen minutes of hiking, we've passed several of the little "burn" piles Kenneth's assembled. But we don't see him.

Worry starts knocking at my ribs. I try to turn her away, not to let her in, but the bitch isn't having it.

"Something's wrong," I whisper. I grip the bullhorn tighter.

We start to walk faster, despite the fact that our feet brush against the leaves and we make more noise. The leaves, my breath, the wind, and those damned parrots screeching, "You can't cum yet, shithead!"—the noises start to blur. My eyes scan back and forth, at first methodically and then more frantically as we keep going and there's no sign of Kenneth.

Alec comes to a dead stop in front of me and I nearly trip over him. He reaches out a hand to help me and I grab a nearby tree in order to keep my balance.

There, on the path in front of us, is Kenneth. He's lying on the ground, face down.

Everything inside me curls up into fetal position. This can't be happening. I shake my head side to side. "No!"

Alec bends down and rolls Kenneth over.

There's a massive bump on my chef's forehead, but he's not shot. He's not dead. I scan his body quickly. The rest of him looks intact and uninjured. Thank fuck.

"His gun's gone," Alec growls, standing up and immediately pulling his own weapon, turning in a slow circle and surveying the trees.

I crouch down and touch Kenneth's face, careful to avoid the obvious injury.

"Kenneth, can you hear me?"

He moans, but doesn't respond. At least he's alive.

"Peter," Alec and I say at the same time.

That slimy little turd. I clench my fingers and swallow hard, focusing back on Kenneth. I try to smack back my sadness at seeing him hurt, at knowing he was betrayed. I can't break down. I need to focus on the plan. Focus on the plan.

When Alec is sure that Peter the bastard is gone, he crouches down and does his own check on Kenneth. "He's out."

"I noticed."

Alec runs his hands over Kenneth, checking him. "I think he'll be okay. I hope. Guess Peter stole his gun."

My stomach wrings itself out like a dishrag at Alec's words and I nearly vomit at the thought that Kenneth might not be okay. God, we need to see if Heather and Andrew and the others are still here. If they're okay. We need to take care of Kenneth—he needs a doctor—we need— I spot the penis piñata through the trees, just feet away. Kenneth never got it in position. Shit. We need that for tonight. It's a major part of our plan.

I tromp over and retrieve it. I use the string attached to the tip and wrap it around my shoulders and torso a few times until the piñata settles between my shoulder blades like a backpack. A giant penis backpack. I take deep, deliberate breaths, trying to keep myself calm. I can't freak out. It's not the time to freak out.

Alec interrupts my thoughts by handing me his gun. "You guard rear?"

"You think Peter Brown's gonna be a problem?"

Alec shakes his head. "Nah. He's too scared to go approach those Russians himself. He's gonna hide in the trees again. You got rear?" he repeats.

I nod. We make it halfway back to my villa when Kenneth stirs in Alec's arms. I jog forward and grab his hand just before he opens his eyes.

"Kenneth!" I laugh-cry in relief.

But then he says, "Grandma?" and I want to laugh-cry for a whole different reason.

"Pretty bad concussion," Alec diagnoses when Kenneth springs out of his arms and goes to puke on a nearby tree.

I nod. Fuck! It could be so much worse but ... fuck!

Kenneth turns around and sways on his feet. "Is it chicken pot pie tonight? I love chicken pot—"

Alec has to scoop him up before he face plants.

Our trek resumes.

My hand fidgets on the bullhorn I carry, and every twig cracking sends me spinning, gun raised. I'm on edge. I swallow back the bile that builds up inside my throat as reality hits.

We're about to attack armed Russian mobsters. And our little group is down to two.

CHAPTER TWENTY

HEATHER

Thank fuck I took that crystal. Because these dumbasses are too smart for their own good. Or for my good, I guess. They solve puzzles that unlock the window compartments in the hallway so they can reach in and get the containers and potion ingredients inside. Then they solve puzzles associated with those items, which open up a damned beehive-looking receptacle where they can shove all the rainbow crystals. The Russians get them in, but they're missing one very important crystal.

I try real hard to look confused.

I try real hard to look like I'm helping search.

J2, ever the suspicious asshole, tells me to sit the fuck down.

I watch them nervously as they turn the escape room upside down, turning everything over and moving it and eventually, somehow, fucking us over so that we're left in the dark. Who knows what idiot pulled what cord to make that happen? I'm just glad it happened. I lean against the wall in my spot on the floor—glad I can finally look smug without getting noticed—while they all pull out their cell phones and try to solve two problems by flashlight. Plug in the cord. Find the crystal. Their little lights dance around the floor as they crawl on hands and knees. The only other streak of light in the place comes from a small, square skylight.

I stare up at that little bit of freedom while the Russians get increasingly pissed, snapping at each other in two languages.

Damn, I hope they're still this pissed at each other and all distracted when they get out. They'll be easier to rile up and get to whatever spot we need so we can—*Boosh!* I make the noise with my mouth. I fucking wish I had my phone. I consider trying to steal a Russian's, but I'd never get it unlocked. I don't have any phone numbers memorized. Oh—and the writing might be in those funny squiggles. Yeah, not worth it.

Rubin sits down beside me, giving up on the search. He looks at me and follows my gaze.

Suddenly, he stands. "I know how to get out. We need to use the window up there." He points.

The other men look at the skylight.

"No way. We not fit," Blob says.

Damn straight, he won't fit.

But Rubin's insistent. "That's the game, right? Heather's games are all about team building. We work together."

Reval tilts his head and studies the skylight. He waves Rubin over. "Lift me. Let me see what we can do."

So, it becomes a team effort. I bite down on a smile as I

think about how much these dopes look like a bunch of male cheerleaders. Blob goes into a half lunge so that Reval can use his thigh as a step up to Rubin's shoulders. J2 holds Reval's hands for balance, and Suity keeps his hands spread behind Reval's ass, to catch him in case he falls.

Damn. What a time to be without a phone. The Instagram world will forever miss out on this pathetic, sliding, curse-filled gymnastics session.

After three glorious failed attempts that practically make me piss myself, Reval is finally up, hands braced against the ceiling, pulling on the latch that keeps the skylight shut. He can't get it open by hand, so he puts his hand down and one of the other idiots hands him a gun. He uses the handle to smash the latch.

I fucking book it for a hallway when he starts that shit. He's gonna accidentally shoot—and he does. *Pow!* The bullet ricochets around the room, sending all the guys ducking and Reval falling flat onto Rubin's back.

I roll my eyes at their idiocy. But do they give up and try another solution? Nope. Because they're men. They repeat the entire dumb process over. The only thing they change is that this time, Reval uses one of the big, magnetic rectangles from the games to beat at the latch. He is—surprisingly—successful. He gets the window to unlatch. But when Rubin and the others use their hands to try to boost him through, he doesn't fit.

Not a shock, considering he's roughly the size of a frickin' grizzly bear.

He climbs down and they try to boost up Suity. No go. J2's shoulders are even more massive than the other guys, and even if Blob's shoulders would fit, his stomach definitely won't.

After they've exhausted all their options, they turn and look at me.

"Hell no," I say. "I am not a fan of heights."

"You go out, unlock the door and let us out, then maybe after you sign papers, we say you slipped away. Or maybe we take just fingernail, a lock of hair, to prove you are gone?" J2 thinks he's being persuasive.

Pull off my fucking fingernails? Trash my hair? Hell to the no. I'd rather they just fucking kill me. 'Course, I'm not dumb enough to say that. Because there's still the possibility of the bomb.

If they let me out, and I can get word to the guys, maybe we can find a way to get that fucking thing back here and drop it through the skylight. That could work.

I try not to let my thoughts show on my face as I run through the scenarios, picturing this building transforming into a beautiful orange fireball.

Thank fucking goodness the lights went out, is all I gotta say. My face would give me dead away right now.

I clear my throat and try and sound reluctant as I climb to my feet. "You promise? You promise, if I get you out and sign over the money ... you'll let me go?"

J2 puts his hand up in devil horns, turns his fingers inward and smacks himself on the chest. "I promise." Is he swearing on the devil or something? What the fuck?

I do not have time to analyze the weirdness. I wanna get out of here and see Andrew and those other schmucks. So, I just nod.

The guys shove me up onto J2's shoulders, and I stretch upward. I press on the skylight. The latch is undone but the glass itself has flipped back down and the skylight is closed. The guys all pushed it open with no issue when they tried to squish through. But I'm not quite as tall and I don't have quite their upper body strength.

I shove against the glass. I smack my palms harder against it and it starts to budge. But I need a better angle because it opens on the left side and I'm too centered. I shift my legs, widening my stance. But shit—that makes the crystal in my ass start to slip. Fuck. I clench my cheeks the best I can, but I'm cocked to one side right now and I can't maintain a good grip on it. I punch the glass hard and the crystal slides a little further down. I can feel it prairie dogging, the tip popping out of my ass. But at that moment, the skylight swings open like the page of a book and smacks against the roof.

I'm almost there.

"Push me up more!" I urge.

J2 shoves his left hand up, lifting my left foot and spreading my legs further apart. The crystal slips and it's halfway out. I push down on J2's left hand and shift my weight to that side as my hands grasp the edges of the window frame. Another slip. But it's fine. It's still in there.

"Jump!" I command.

J2 jumps, giving me the extra height I need to get my elbows braced on top of the window frame. I swing my right leg up and awkwardly lodge my foot on the back corner of the skylight. Then I lean forward onto my elbows and bring my left foot up catty-corner. My plan is to launch myself forward. The roof is flat, so at worst, I'll get scratched up. I tense my legs, and shove. I frog-leap forward—I guess the movement is too much. The crystal shoots out of my ass and falls down, down, down.

"She shit onto me. She shit onto me!" J2's wail comes up through the skylight. As I fly through the sky like an awkward, over-sized, flying fucking squirrel, I hear a *ping*. The crystal hits the ground inside.

I land clumsily next to the skylight, cursing the trainer Shane Paul used to send me to. I mean, what the fuck? I should more than be able to do cheerleading moves and leap out of skylights after the squats he put me through. Fuck him. He's a goddamned liar and I'm gonna sue his pants off when I get home.

My internal cursing is overridden as cursing floats up through the skylight.

"Is not shit! It is missing crystal!" Suity McGunpants exclaims.

Aw, fuck.

A shot sounds and a bullet flies up through the skylight and into the orange sky. Guess the Russians are back to thinking we're on opposite sides.

Dammit all. Now I really have to run and warn the guys, "The Russians are coming, the Russians are coming!"

I scramble away from the skylight and look for a way down

from the roof, but this ain't America. Fire escapes aren't required. Shitballs.

I hear a creak and scramble over to the edge of the roof. I peer down and see the gun-toting bastards leaving the building.

Fucking hell! I'm stuck! Andrew and the guys are gonna be hit without warning. And I just pissed these assholes off something fierce. I have to warn the guys. I glance around the roof, wondering how the hell I'm gonna do that.

There are a couple of half-brown, rotten mangoes off to one side. I lunge for them and take aim. I throw those mother-fuckers rapid-fire at the gangsters below. The first one goes wide. The second is short. The third mango smacks J2 in the back.

I duck immediately, but I still feel the gunfire as it zooms over my head. My ears ring from the sound the shots. *Crack-thump. Crack-thump. Crack-thump.* I cover my head with my hands and press my cheek into the roof. I can only hope the shots are enough of a warning for Andrew and the others.

"You are dead woman!" J2 screams up at me.

Holy shit. Guess this war is officially starting.

We'd better win.

CHAPTER TWENTY-ONE

KATIE

I'm opening the door to my villa for Alec and Kenneth when I hear a loud sound in the distance. A *bang* or a *pop* or something. But it's muffled. I'm not sure exactly what it is.

Alec swallows hard and turns to me. "We need to hurry."

Kenneth's no help as we gather supplies; he's like a broken record, or a kid on a car trip.

"How did I get here?" he asks.

"We carried you after Peter hit you." I say, stuffing my pockets full of a few last-ditch-effort items, just in case.

"Oh. He hit me?" Kenneth looks shocked.

"Yes," Alec had responded the first time the question was asked, while he was using some of my hand sanitizer to try to disinfect the little trickle of blood down Kenneth's temple. "We think he hit you with his walking stick."

"I must have a hard head. Maybe I'm a superhero," Kenneth

had said before flinching. "We should sue the head company. I need a harder head. Mine's broken."

Every minute or two, the cycle would restart, with Kenneth sitting up a little straighter, staring around, and asking how he got here.

After the fifth cycle, Alec pulls me aside. "We can't bring him."

I nod. "I know."

"We need to keep him safe though."

I know what he's asking me to do, without him needing to say it aloud. I go over to one of the boxes we raided earlier and pull out a roll of duct tape.

We tape Kenneth loosely—he's so out of it that he just kind of watches us do it. I feel guilty, but it's safer for him and for us if he stays out of sight.

Alec lifts Kenneth up and carries him into the closet while he babbles on about lawsuits.

He doesn't even protest when we set him on the closet floor and start to stack boxes around him.

"Isn't there someone we can sue? We should sue someone," Kenneth insists, grabbing at my wrist.

Alec hands me the last of the water bottles from my villa and I pry myself out of Kenneth's grasp to open the lid, placing it within his reach. I lean forward and give him a kiss on the uninjured side of his forehead, ignoring his babbling.

I stand and take a deep breath, steadying myself and

adjusting the giant penis that's still tied onto my back—it slid down a little as I settled Kenneth. When I have the paper dick where I like it, Alec and I walk back out to the living room. I can see the sunset through the shattered window. It's gorgeous; orange and pink swathes of color dance through the sky.

Alanis Morissette's *Isn't it Ironic* starts to play in my head. It figures that we'll fight for our lives under a beautiful tropical sunset.

It's time to move.

That's when we hear the gunshots. Three in a row. Not muffled bangs. Not muted pops. Loud, angry gunshots.

I freeze. My limbs lock. Alec turns to stare at me.

My stupid ostrich reaction is back. I should duck and cover. I should run. I should do something, but I'm frozen, wide-eyed, my heart as fast as a jackrabbit on speed.

Alec grabs my shoulders and shakes me a little. "Come on, Katie. Grab the vases."

Right. Right. On autopilot, I grab a box of glass vases. Instead of filling them with glass beads and flowers, like I'd intended when I bought them, they're full of tiki oil and strips of washcloths. Improv molotov cocktails.

Alec tucks the last few lighters into his pocket, cocks his gun in one hand, and carries our bullhorn in the other.

"Still got your remote?" I ask.

"Yup. Still got yours?"

I nod.

We head out the door to find out what the hell is going down and hopefully, maybe, possibly fuck some shit up.

Except, what the hell do we find when we start walking?

Angry Russian mobsters, which we were expecting. Only, they're running the wrong way, yelling and snarling at one another as they do. They're running away from the runway, away from the escape room building, and toward the rest of the villas. In the exact opposite direction of the one we wanted them to go.

Alec and I exchange a look. Instead of starting fires like we'd planned, we follow them, slinking from tree to tree, but trying to match their hurried pace.

Hopefully, we can find out what the heck is going on and why they are so freaked out.

There are three Russians—the same three I saw climb out of the helicopter. But where are the other two? The twins follow the Russians, arguing in low voices with one another.

"Wasn't that helicopter a six-seater?" I ask Alec.

He does a quick head count. "If they planned on taking the twins back with them, maybe this is it. Maybe there aren't two more hiding."

I latch onto Alec's theory. I glare at the twins' backs. Those back-stabbing, disgusting, underwear model lookalikes. I wish eternal crotch rot on them for tricking me. I hope they get all the STDs ever discovered until their dicks shrivel up like gummy worms.

The Russians barrel past the pool and head straight for the back door of the kitchen, the one that the staff uses. It's propped open just a bit. The two big Russians stop, raising their guns toward the door. The largest one, the Hulk of the group—Gunmetal George, who searched our closet—jerks his head at the chubby one to open it.

Chubby Bunny yanks open the door and then screams bloody murder. He turns back around. His face and clothes are somehow stained brown. I hear a clang and my eyes fall down to see a coffee pot rolling away.

Someone must have propped up hot coffee on the door. Homemade alarm system.

Chubby Bunny is moaning and stripping off his clothes as fast as he can—trying to get the hot liquid away from his skin. His man boobs jiggle as he shimmies out of his pants. Pink burn marks pop up all over the front of his face and torso.

The Russians all take a step back from him.

Chubby Bunny ignores them all and runs right for the pool. He jumps in.

Apparently that's a bad idea, because he just screams all over again and scrambles back out. Guess chlorine and burn wounds don't mix well. He limps to the bar and starts chugging vodka.

One gunmen down. And we didn't even have to do anything. Now we're two versus four. Four monster-sized men. But still.

Chubby Bunny swipes a hand over his mouth and moans. "This was to be easy pick up. Simple kidnap."

"Shut up," Suit tells his burnt companion as he circles the

kitchen on the pool side. His gun is up and he's on high alert.

Gunmetal George goes behind the door and tries to peer through the crack by the doorjamb. He squints into the kitchen. I assume he's searching for more improvised weapons.

His search, combined with the coffee pot on top of the door, can only mean one thing. Hope leaps in my chest like a pink ballerina. Heather and her guys are still here. Still fighting. It's not just Alec and I alone. My hand reaches out and grabs Alec's wrist. I lean up and whisper my theory.

He nods, eyes focused on the Russians as they near the kitchen doorway.

BOOOOOOOM!

There's an explosion from the kitchen and the Russians are thrown to the ground. The force billows out, blasting open the door and busting the windows. I can feel the heat and hot wind push past me.

My ears ring, so I set down my box of molotov vases and I crouch down. I use my hands to cup my ears and muffle the sound. Smoke billows out of the kitchen door, and the awful smell of fire and burning plastic permeates the air.

When I uncup my hands, I hear someone mutter a curse beside me. But it doesn't come from Alec.

Fuck! Was our assumption wrong? Are there more Russians?

My throat dries out. I turn ... and see the three guys left in

Heather's harem competition standing and watching the kitchen casually, as if a burning building was no big deal.

"Dammit! Didn't take out a' one of them. I knew I shoulda' set that timer for another five minutes!" Jeremiah Bible shakes his head. He must have walked up while I was dazed from the explosion. He's wearing an apron—only an apron —and he's taped a magnetic kitchen knife strip to his chest with duct tape. It's covered in cleavers. His brown hair is wild. He looks like he's from a very scary, very cheap horror flick. He spits through the gap in his front teeth at the Russians. A little bit of spit lands on his chin. I revise my impression, he looks like he's from *Scary Movie 10*.

Next to him are Andrew and BJ. They are wearing loin-cloths made of white string and kitchen towels. The hot barbarian look is kind of ruined by the prints that Kenneth has on his kitchen towels. Andrew's got a screen-printed whisk on the front towel. Above the whisk is written: "Beat It." And BJ's kitchen towel is sporting a cake piping bag illustration that says, "Just the tip."

It would be a photo-worthy moment if life weren't so fucked up.

The other two men don't look nearly as crazy or dangerous as Jeremiah, though. Andrew carries a sawed-off oven cleaning canister and a bleach spray bottle. BJ carries some pie pans and a flashlight.

I look past the guys and search the trees, but I don't see anyone else. Just the three of them. I blink hard and blow out a breath. I try not to let the rising tide of fear and disappointment wash out my voice as I ask, "Where's Heather?"

Andrew flicks his eyes over to me. "She was distracting them. Where have you been?"

"Setting up traps," Alec responds for me. "Know why they fired earlier?"

Andrew shakes his head and his voice cracks when he answers me. "They've been with Heather for hours."

A sinkhole opens in my stomach and my heart drops into it. Shit. Those gunshots.

I dig my fingernails into my palms.

Alec puts a hand on my shoulders. "Let's smoke those moth-erfuckers." He pulls out a lighter and places it in one of my hands. Then he grabs a vase and puts it in the other hand.

I light it, letting my anger guide me, not listening as Alec fills the others in on the plan to drive the Russians toward the runway.

They nod and BJ pulls out his flashlight as I launch the burning vase in the air.

The vase hits the wall of the kitchen building, exploding into flames that drip down the side. Suit has an automatic reaction and fires at the sound. He narrowly misses Gunmetal George, who yells at him. The twins come running back around the corner to see what the commotion is. Once they see the broken glass and the fire, they start talking in rapid-fire Russian with the others.

Watching them talk amps up my anxiety. "We should do something," I whisper to Alec. "We need to keep them off balance. We can't give them time to plan."

"On it," BJ aims his flashlight at George's ass and waves for all of us to scoot sideways. Why? I don't really know, but Alec helps me pick up my box, straighten the piñata, and walk about twenty feet to the south, toward the runway. BJ flicks the flashlight on, only I don't see a burst of white light like I expect. Instead, a small red beam cuts through the trees. Did they modify the flashlight? What the hell is it? A laser?

Seconds later, Gunmetal George shrieks and grabs at his ass, where his pants smoke slightly. He smacks at the pant-legs, turns, and starts shooting into the trees.

BJ immediately drops and rolls, like a pro ninja. I guess that laser pointer's more than just a laser light.

The trees behind BJ eat bullets—Gunmetal's aim is far too good for my liking. He's only a foot or two off-target, even with an obstructed view.

Crap. He's way too good a marksman.

Gunmetal George takes cover behind the open kitchen door and yells around the side of the building to Suit and Chubby Bunny. Chubby's swaying too much to stand, but Suit comes trotting over and the two of them eye the tree line cautiously.

"Fuck yeah, motherfuckers! We've got a laser-gun. Bring it, bitches!" Jeremiah whispers as he fist pumps and high fives BJ, who's joined us.

Andrew just stares at the Russians as the sun slips down beyond the horizon, his eyes tight and jaw clenched. I can practically feel him radiating hatred. Alec pulls him by the shoulder and they start walking toward our goal, stomping loudly and making noise, hoping to draw the Russians in our direction. I start to follow but something makes me stop. Intuition? Stupidity? Who knows?

I set down my box and start unwrapping the piñata on my back. Tingles travel up my spine. I have a feeling Gunmetal George is like Heather. I have this gut instinct that he's not one to take humiliation lightly. I have a feeling he's gonna come at us with everything he's got, because he isn't capable of backing down. He looks like the kind of guy who'd rather get shot than get humiliated. I don't think burning his ass was the best idea. I think we've just poked the bear too much.

I watch the Russians as I light the rope at the end of the piñata and climb into the trees so I can launch it down the little slope of hill toward them. When I'm up in the tree, I see a couple of gathering thunder clouds in the distance. Crap. I hope they don't get big lightning storms down here. Or big winds. Or anything like that. We'd better hurry.

I fumble around and eventually wedge the giant paper dick between two branches, using the balls to keep it stuck in place. I light it and I scurry down as the fuse burns down to nothing, scratching my arm on the bark as I try to hurry.

My heart thumps in my chest as I grab a couple Molotov cocktails to run with me.

I glance backward and see Gunmetal George handing guns to each of the twins. His face promises darkness and pain. Suit comes up next to him and hands out charred cutting boards from the kitchen, which they all hold up as shields.

Those motherfuckers come charging into the forest, teeth bared, right at me.

And I ostrich again as my mind whirls. My eyes shut and I just send out panic signals to the universe. S.O.S. Someone save us, please!

But there's no answering lightning strike to topple them.

My eyes open and ostrich mode flicks off, letting out that little rage monster I've only ever felt once before. I kick the box of vases over, letting the cocktails roll down the hill, because carrying them is gonna slow me down too much. I turn and run.

The dick bursts into flame behind me as I zig-zag through the trees. Fireworks shoot in every direction. Pops of blue and yellow and green fill the air.

The Russians shriek behind me. I look back. One of the twins flaps his arm up and down, waving a flaming sleeve. The other one stops to help him yank his shirt off and then drop and roll. But when he stands, his arm is limp at his side.

Good, the fireworks at least made it harder for one of their shooters.

I risk a second glance behind me and realize my mistake. Because while the fireworks might startle them, make them duck and cover, even hurt them, the damned things light up the night. And when I look back that second time, Gunmetal George's eyes are locked on me.

CHAPTER TWENTY-TWO

HEATHER

It was boring as fuck being stuck on the roof. That's why I climbed back down through the skylight just as soon I was certain those Russian limp dicks were gone. I let myself dangle from the ceiling and drop and roll. Still hurts like a motherfucker half an hour later.

I think about following the Russians, but I can't do much to help the guys when I don't have a weapon. And the escape room doesn't have jack shit in terms of weapons.

Which is why I'm in the maintenance hangar for the airplanes. I've already tucked a flare gun into my pocket and I'm searching the place for other shit.

And fuck me sideways, unless I want to hit the Russians over the head with a wrench, or knock them backward with a power washer, I'm screwed. I sit down on the ground to pout and end up staring at a coil of thin metal wire. I don't know what the hell it's used for. But immediately, I think of *Home Alone*. I think trip wire. Maybe if I can't attack, I can at least give myself some advance notice when the jerkwads come back. I stand up and grab the wire. Then I grab a couple boxes of screws and toss them in a bucket. Because you know what? If it worked for Kevin McCallister ...

I set out toward the tree line, aware that there are some deep grey clouds rolling closer. Maybe that will make those assholes hole up for the night. They are a bunch of pussies after all, and kitties hate the rain. But I don't stop.

I'm just finishing up when I hear an explosion. I perk up. Did it work? Did it fucking work?

I stand and turn, even though I can't see jack through the trees.

But I hear gunshots in the distance. No!

Fuck! Andrew!

My inner beast howls and I stand up and bolt forward.

I get caught on my own damn tripwire and go sprawling. My head smacks the ground. Shit! I feel dizzy. I feel like I'm seeing double. Or hallucinating.

I feel like I'm seeing a helicopter in the distance ...

CHAPTER TWENTY-THREE

KATIE

Gunmetal George is bearing down on me. My legs are burning, my lungs are burning, my hands are shaking as I light another cocktail. I hold it against my chest as I run, ignoring the pain of the little flame against me. I can't throw it until it's burnt a little more. What if I miss? What if he shoots?

I dodge right. I can hear him behind me. I have to dodge bushes—Gunmetal is so huge, he just smashes right through them.

For some ungodly reason—Kenny Loggins' "This is It" starts playing in my head. I hate that song. My mother always used to play it and sing along while she did the dishes. Now, as tree branches smack me in the face and I'm worried about a bullet hitting me in the base of my spine—I don't get any badass, motivational beat. Nope, my brain provides seventies crap. Is this my death knell? Is the universe trying to get me to give up?

Ominous thunder cracks in the distance.

Great. Really funny, universe. Awesome. It was a dark and stormy night ...

I duck right behind a fat tree and lob that fucking Molotov cocktail as hard as I can. It doesn't hit a tree. It smacks harmlessly on the ground and the glass doesn't break. Because— of course not. I want to laugh and cry in the same moment.

Gunmetal just leaps over the vase and keeps running.

Dammit. I don't have time for the second cocktail. I drop that vase. I reach for my pocket and pull out the tube of prank itching powder Heather had wanted. "Just for shits and giggles," she'd said. "Like, if one of them is really annoying."

I decide shooting at me classifies as annoying as I uncap the powder and edge around the side of the tree so I can get an eye on Gunmetal George.

I don't see him.

Fuck!

I turn back to look the other way only to find myself facing the barrel of a gun. My eyes widen and I pee a tiny bit.

Gunmetal gives a scary grin and licks his lips, in total creeper fashion.

My heart pops like a balloon. I shriek, throwing my arms up and tossing itching powder all over the both of us.

Gunmetal sneezes, but doesn't seem to react otherwise. His hands stay firmly planted on the gun as I take half a step back.

"Do not move—" he says. But then he starts sliding his teeth over his tongue. And his hand reaches up to scratch the side of his face.

I'd be smug, only I'm feeling it too. It feels like ants are crawling in my hair. I reach up and dig in with my nails. It itches so much it burns. I have the urge to scratch until I bleed—just to stop the itch.

I peel off Danny's shirt. God, that feels better! I don't even care that I'm topless in front of the enemy. But my hair. My hair. I can't stop scratching.

Gunmetal rips his shirt off. He's more ripped than shredded newspaper. Fuck. He reaches for me, even as he scratches a bloody streak into his own cheek with the butt of his gun.

Suddenly, out of nowhere, a metal pie plate comes zooming through the air and hits Gunmetal in the face. It slices his good cheek open. Now he really looks like a horror movie villain.

I'm dazed for a second. Out of it. Since when are pie plates sharp?

Andrew runs up beside me with a spray bottle. "Katie, run!" He spritzes something at Gunmetal. And the scent of bleach fills the air.

Gunmetal howls in pain.

I howl in itchiness as I run away, still scratching.

I glance back. Gunmetal backhands Andrew, who flies through the air, but just keeps spraying. It looks like he might hit one of the twins in the eyes, because one of them sinks to the ground, clutching at his face.

Yeah! Andrew's a badass!

As soon as I think that, I realize I can't see Suit. Shit.

I see a cleaver zoom through the air past me and bite into the tree next to Suit as he tries to grab me.

"Katie!" Alec yells.

I run toward the sound of Alec's voice, zig-zagging through the trees as a couple shots zing back and forth around me. I can't tell if it's the Russians shooting at us or us shooting at them, but nobody screams, so I take it as a good sign.

A hand wraps around me and I turn, ready to fall sobbing into Alec's arms in relief.

But it's not Alec who's grabbed me. It's Peter Brown.

His eyes glint coldly as he yanks me backward and puts Kenneth's old gun to my neck. He closes one hand over my arms and frog marches me back to R&R.

I should feel fear. I should feel disappointment. I should feel idiotic for getting caught and frog-marched topless through the forest. Those are all my normal Katie feelings for a humiliating situation like this. An almost-getaway. But maybe I've reached my limit. Maybe I'm all feeled out.

I just stare dully at the twins as Peter says, "You want her? You want them? You want to know everything they've got planned?"

The right twin, the one with the burnt arm, says, "What do you want?"

"I want fifty grand in unmarked bills."

Fuck. He's gonna give away the guys. Alec will get hurt. Our whole plan rests on him staying a stealth sniper.

I wrench myself away from Peter and shove my hands to cover his mouth. We wrestle and I bend his wrist backward. Guess I should have gone for the gun. Because it goes off.

CHAPTER TWENTY-FOUR

HEATHER & KATIE

Heather

I blink. I think I must be imagining things. I see a helicopter land on the runway, blades whirring. I see gunmen jump out. But we already have gunmen we're fighting ...

Katie

The bullet hits Peter in the ass. How he manages to shoot his own ass, I have no fucking clue. But my fingers did not pull the damn trigger. I do mentally give the universe a quick thumbs up before darting into the trees again, scratching frantically at my head as I run ... *smack!* Right back into Gunmetal George's massive pecs ...

Heather

These gunmen are different. I push up onto my elbow and try to focus as I see them. Everything is definitely blurry, so I blink hard. These gunmen are backlit by a spotlight on their chopper, and rain starts to fall, distorting their features, but their edges are different, somehow. It takes me a minute to realize that they aren't wearing suits like the Russians. They're wearing leather jackets...

Katie

"You've got to be kidding," I moan as Gunmetal scoops me up over his shoulder. It's massive, almost as wide as Jeremy's old motorcycle seat. Ugh.

To my surprise, Gunmetal turns to Suit and says, "We go back to this way," and jerks his head toward the escape room. He scratches his chest as he explains, "They will not have time to leave the bombs there. We out wait the storm."

Suit nods.

And then the Russians leave behind a sobbing Peter Brown and head exactly in the direction we wanted them to go.

Heather

I stand on wobbly feet and wave my arms. One guy draws his gun, but doesn't point it. The other guys simply eye me, until one takes the initiative and steps forward. He's got black hair, a large hooked nose, and a thick, solid body under his black biker outfit.

"Yo, you in trouble or somethin'?"

He sounds like he's from the East Coast.

I swallow and it's a minute before I can find my voice. "Yeah. I am. Who are you?"

When he says he's a warlock, I crack up.

I'm definitely hallucinating. These guys can't be real. I musta' hit my head harder than I thought ...

Katie

Yes, just a little farther. I squirm on Gunmetal's shoulders. My purpose is two-fold. Get more damned rain on my hair because it's washing away the itch powder, and get access to my damned pocket.

"Stop this," Gunmetal growls at me.

"Sorry, I gotta pee," I lie.

"I have heard that trick before."

"You have?" I ask, as I slide my hand into my now available pocket. Inside, I finger the remote control for the spotlights I hung in the trees. Damn. I hope Alec and the guys are ready. Because, ready or not ...

Heather

The man in the leather jacket grabs my arm. "You okay?" he asks.

I say the first damn thing that pops into my head. "There are men trying to kill me—"

Great, Heather! That makes you seem batshit! I scold myself as Hook Nose backs away. "I'll blow you if you help me!" I promise desperately.

That offer does not help the cause. Fuck it.

I'm about to pull out my flare gun and hold him hostage when spotlights flood the area. Immediately, all the dudes in leather pull out guns. They start firing at the shadows that encircle us.

Katie

Gunmetal drops me on the ground when the lights pop up, illuminating a bunch of scary, sex doll silhouettes. He takes a knee and opens fire on a group of them to his left. One of them lets out a loud squeak. One pops and I see him jerk his head, like he's wondering what the hell just happened. Luckily, the rain decides to bitch slap him—come on, Universe!—and pour down in sheets just then, so Gunmetal doesn't question, just keeps emptying his magazine and replacing it with a new one from his pants pocket.

I'm about to try to creep away when I see movement to our right. What the hell? There's another helicopter? And more gunmen! Holy shit! Do the Russians have backup? My plan is fucked!

Gunmetal turns.

Suddenly, everyone's firing at everyone. I drop to the ground and army crawl the fuck away, ignoring how much that hurts my bare breasts. What the hell is going on?

Heather

I am about to book it when Hook grabs me around the waist and bellows across the landing strip, "You want this chick? Drop your weapons or I'll kill her myself!"

Oh shit. This did not go as planned. He's supposed to be my hero, not another spermbag douche.

Something moves in the distance and then a person flies, literally flies, right at us. All the warlocks open fire.

The figure falls and Hook drags me over to look at it.

"Congratulations. They made you waste your ammo killing a sex doll." Idiot.

I realize I'm gonna have to save myself.

I try to kick him in the balls, but I miss. Maybe because he doesn't have any. Dumbass coward who's using a woman as a shield. I reach for my flare gun—

Katie

OMFG! Those other guys have Heather! For a second, I wonder if I've been shot. No. It's just shock. Just utter disbelief zinging through me and ripping my insides apart.

I shove aside my wet, tangled hair and try to get a better look at the dickwads who grabbed Heather—the grease-lightning gang or whoever the hell they are—dressed all in black. They don't sound Russian. But, maybe they're a rival gang? Maybe that's why they're shooting at each other?

Well, fuck them! I reach for my trusty remote again and press a button; this time, all my colored lights go to work.

Come on, Alec. Be here—

Heather

I'm kicking and screaming and bucking as Hook Nose tries to drag me toward his chopper. I get my hand in place on the trigger of the flare gun.

But blue and red flashing lights start up all around us. I freeze. So does Hook Nose.

"Put your hands in the air! This is the police! Drop your weapons and put your hands in the air!" a deep voice growls through a bullhorn.

Hook Nose and his crew look over at the Russians. There's

a middle-school level stare down, until I interrupt it, screaming, "You all used up all your damn bullets already, so unless you're ready for suicide by cop—drop them!"

Like most men in the face of my brutal honesty—Katie calls it my Hurricane voice—they fucking listen.

Damn straight they do.

I drop my flare gun, too. And step away from Hook, my hands raised. I do not want a fucking cop to shoot through me to get to him.

Only ... we stand there waiting, hands up.

And no one comes out.

What the hell?

Katie

Oh, God. I never thought this plan would work! Honestly, I never thought we'd get that far. Shit! The rainfall has let up, but it feels deafening in the expectant silence. I can hear my pulse pounding in my ears as I swallow hard. Next are supposed to be the confetti cannons. But they don't go off. They're supposed to be a loud noise, a distraction so we can run out and swipe up the weapons and Alec can snipe people. But there are too many people now. And no sound. The rain ... I think the rain might have melted the confetti into paper pulp. Shit! Shit! Shit!

Heather

Hook Nose screams, "It's a fake!" And all the assholes dive to the ground for their weapons.

I dive for mine.

Katie

Thunder crashes and the wind blows so hard it goes sideways, slapping me in the face. Okay, Universe, I get it. I done fucked up. Gonna die now. Thanks.

But then that whirring turns into a different noise. A sound I've heard before. A sound that I once thought was a tsunami.

I look up at the sky and a third helicopter hovers over the runway.

Are you joking? Who the fuck—

A machine gun fires a line of bullets down onto the runway, so that dirt and rocks fly up in a little row.

A new voice speaks over a loudspeaker. "Drop those fucking weapons or we will shoot you down one by one. By order of the government of the United fucking States."

Heather

My heart gives a fist pump. Hell yeah! 'Merica! I have no idea who these new fuckwits are, but thank fucking God!

Ropes drop out of the helicopter and seven badass looking men in black ops gear slide down. Damn. That's the hottest sight I've ever seen.

Katie

Holy shit! Is this really happening? This is really happening! I can't help the nervous laughter that erupts when guys with night vision goggles and helmets and all that crap point their guns at the Russians and those other dudes alike. They collect all the weapons and zip-tie all these jerkwads' hands. They pat me down, but since all I've got is a light switch, they don't zip tie me.

Instead, when they see me start to shake—I think shock and cold are setting in—one of them gently leads me over to Heather. He doesn't even comment on the fact that I'm topless and holding my arms over my chest.

"Do you two know each other?" he asks.

"I thought you were dead!" I screech, throwing myself into her arms.

Heather

I hug Katie so hard that I think I might break her ribs. And then, like a fucking baby, I start to cry.

Katie

We get our sobfest on while the army dudes move their prisoners into the airplane hangar. When they emerge, their leader signals for the helicopter to land.

"Um ... wait," a familiar growly voice calls through the trees. "Can the rest of us come out?"

The helicopter searchlight swings to the left, where Alec, Andrew, BJ, and Jeremiah stand at the edge of the trees, arms in the air. Their weapons, as lethal or homemade or ridiculous as they were, are gone. This means, of course, that Jeremiah is buck naked and his johnson is whipping in the wind.

I turn to Heather and shake my head. "When we get off this island, I never want to see another one of your harem member's dicks again."

Heather laughs. "Deal. I'm done with harems anyway."

And she squeezes my hand, lets go, and runs toward the guys, who've all been through pat-down. She launches herself into the air and right into Andrew's arms.

My hand goes to my lips and another set of tears fill my eyes as I watch them. "I picked him," I whisper to myself.

"Yeah, you're pretty good at picking guys," a tenor voice quips behind me.

I whirl around, gasping.

There, drenched in rain, wearing borrowed clothes and a helmet that cocks awkwardly to his left side, is Danny.

CHAPTER TWENTY-FIVE

KATIE

I feel like I can breathe a full breath again. Like maybe, I've accidentally been holding my breath the whole time he's been gone—in that nervous way people do when they're just waiting for something to be over—they get tense and hold their breath. That's what I did while Danny was gone, and I didn't even realize it until now. Until seeing him brings up all the realities of having to live without him, having to hold it together and fight through it all without the person who laughs with me at my side.

I don't so much ugly cry as ugly wail as I leap at Danny. Unlike Heather, I don't stick the landing. There's an awkward jumble of arms and elbows because I am shaking too much to be in full control of my body right now. I don't care. I don't fucking care. I let Danny worry about the not-letting-me fall part as I kiss him.

My kisses are probably full of tears and maybe even snot. But you know what? He can deal with it. And scold me for it. And laugh at me for it. Because he's here.

Danny kisses me back, just as full of tears as I am, until something makes him laugh. I have no clue what. But his laugh makes me laugh and pretty soon we're laughing in the rain together.

Someone taps me on the shoulder. I turn to see Alec, waiting patiently, Andrew and Heather at his side.

I untangle myself from Danny, hop down and give Alec a huge hug and then a soft kiss on the cheek. "Thank you."

He nods gruffly and quickly strips off his shirt, covering my chest from view.

Whoops. I'd gotten so cold and numb, I'd kind of forgotten about that.

Alec says, "I'm gonna take these two down to check on Kenneth—"

"We can come, too!" I volunteer.

"Nah. Grab some fresh clothes. And don't you have some umbrellas in boxes somewhere?"

I nod.

"Get those. These guys say they won't take off again until the storm lets up. They're gonna take injured first, then the Russians, then Warlocks."

"Wait," Heather stops him. "Those guys are really wizards?"

Danny interjects, "Warlocks—that's their gang name. They're that gang Peter was trying to hide from. From what they said, he owes them closer to a mil. Ran some kinda gambling scam. They were more than happy to come down here to collect him—"

"Wait, you called those crazies?" Heather cocks her hip.

Danny settles his arm over my shoulders. "Oh, yeah. I called them."

"What?"

"Well, I got kinda desperate trying to find someone to come out here. There are no local police, since this is a private island. No other nearby countries wanted to help, the military said a big hell no—"

"Wait, what?" I turn to look up at him. Danny totally looks like he's wearing Seal team shit or something. "Who are those guys then?"

"Well, I ended up calling my brother, who knew a guy. These are ex-special forces. Private hire."

Next to me, Heather blows a raspberry. "The government wouldn't rescue me? Ohh, I feel some big-ass donations going down the drain!"

Danny clears his throat. "Yeah, well, you might want to reconsider donations."

"Why?" She gives him her signature, 'what the hell, you weirdo' look.

"Well, you kinda owe the Black Sharks twenty-four million for this rescue."

Her jaw drops. "Shit! Twenty-four mil?"

I anticipate a hurricane any moment, so I reach out and put a hand on her arm.

She glances over and smiles at me. "What? It's totally worth it." She winks.

I giggle and Danny scoops up my hand.

Heather tugs Alec and Andrew and leads them away. "Let's go check on Kenneth." She turns and walks backward for a second, looking at me. "If I don't hear you having hot reunion sex, I'm gonna be disappointed, young lady!" she yells.

Every fucking eye turns to stare at me. Dammit, Heather! I flush and try to hide behind my hands.

"Oh no," Danny says, pulling my hand down and then sweeping me up into his arms, bridal style. "This time, Hurricane Heather and I agree."

DANNY BRINGS me to his villa, since it's closer. He refuses to let me walk.

"But you've got to be exhausted," I protest, tracing the bags under his eyes gently as he carries me through the rain. The storm has settled down into a tiny drizzle.

"Nope, I'm good."

"Lie." I smile up at him.

It's hard to see his smile back as we walk further onto the path, away from the chaos behind us. The Black Sharks have decided to confiscate the Warlock's helicopter and the prisoners are being loaded aboard as they protest.

"What's gonna happen to those dicks?" I ask Danny.

He shrugs. "Meh. They typically hand those jerks over to the cops. I'm sure there's plenty of shit they can get charged with, I told my brother Heather would pay for him to dig up all kinds of dirt. So, who knows exactly what's gonna happen to them? But I can tell you what's gonna happen to my dick."

"Yeah?" I grin.

He nuzzles my ear. "Oh, yeah."

"Well, I thought you were gonna tell me?"

"You want dirty talk, Katie? Out here in public where anyone can hear us? Damn, you might have Alec's exhibitionist streak," he teases. But then his voice grows husky and he says, "My dick is gonna get hard watching you get naked and play with yourself in front of me. And then my dick is gonna tease your little slit. I'm gonna rub my hot, hard dick up and down over your opening until you're begging me to put it in you. But I'm not gonna."

Shit. Danny can dirty talk. The man can tell a fucking story. Holy mother! I tug on the arm he has cradling my back and grab his hand. I place his fingertips on my nipple.

"Play with me, please," I beg, looping my arms tighter around my neck so I can keep my balance as he does.

He pinches my nipple and starts to gently twist and tug on it as he walks and talks. "I'm gonna make you wait for it, Katie. I'm gonna play with these pretty titties. I'm gonna suck on these nipples and trace your breasts with my tongue. I'm gonna make you beg me to touch you, to bite your nipples, anything to get you a little closer to that edge. But I'm not gonna push you over. I'm gonna head downtown instead. I'm gonna lean you over the arm of my couch, with your hips jutting up so I can see that naughty, wet pussy. And then I'm gonna taste it."

Danny lets go of my nipple and grips my back. He drops my legs and swings my body around so that he's carrying me and I'm facing him, legs wrapped around his waist. He props one hand under my ass and uses the other to slip in front of me, between my legs.

"Katie, I'm gonna eat you out until you are bucking on that couch." His thumb gently circles me, going around and around my clit, touching the edges of it, but never making full contact.

"Danny! Hell! You tease!" I groan.

"You want to come out here in the open?" he whispers, then nibbles on my earlobe.

I moan. I shift and press myself farther onto his finger. "Yes," I breathe.

"What will you give me if I let you come right now?" he asks, his fingers dancing lightly over my clit, giving me almost enough sensation, just not quite.

"Anything," I whisper, leaning up to kiss him.

Our tongues battle for a moment and I try to shove myself harder onto his fingers, but he curls them so I'm simply riding his fist. It's good, but not enough.

Danny breaks the kiss as he kicks open the door to his villa and flicks on a side light. "Anything, huh?"

He carries me in and sets me down at the side of his couch.

"I want a porsche."

I snap my head up and see him smiling. "Lie." I grin.

He gestures for me to take off my clothes. So I strip out of Alec's shirt. I toss down Danny's shorts, and undo my Teva sandals. When I straighten, Danny's eyes widen and he swallows hard.

He steps forward and pulls me into a kiss. His tongue strokes mine gently, almost hesitantly. When he pulls back, his eyes are shining. "You're right. I want this." His hand traces down my neck and settles over my heart.

And that's it. I break apart. Everything I ever thought I wanted fades away. Because I never knew what I didn't know. I've never felt connections like this before.

Danny takes my teary eyes and my tight throat for reluctance. And he quickly stumbles over his words, backtracking. "I don't mean alone. I mean, I'll still share—"

I jump on him and wrap my arms on his neck, tugging him close and clinging to him. "You stupid man. I was just too choked up. Yeah, I mean, you'll share. But you have me. You have me already. You've got my heart."

"I do?" He laughs. And I laugh. And he swings me in a circle.

When he sets me down, I'm pretty sure that the drops on his cheeks aren't just from the rain.

"You're my hero, Danny."

He gives me a cocky grin, one that showcases his dimples. "Oh, I'm about to be. Now, tell me what the first thing I promised to do to you was?"

And just like that, I go from emotional to on fire. My breathing quickens and I repeat, "You were gonna suck my nipples."

"That's right," Danny stalks forward and backs me up until my legs hit the side of the couch. He leans down and takes my right breast in his mouth. His tongue traces up over my nipple and he blades the tip, moving from side to side and flicking until my nipple's at attention. He moves to my other breast and does the same. I want to beg him to suck them, to tease harder, but he takes his tongue down and traces the undersides of my breasts, just like he said he would. And my nipples grow colder and harder, and my mind grows even more desperate for his touch.

"Danny," I plead.

He listens, dragging his mouth up slowly, pressing my breasts together and then flicking his tongue from nipple to nipple. The wet little slaps of his tongue send sensation shooting through me and my pelvis rises to meet his. I can feel how hard he is, how much he loves teasing me. I reach down and put a hand around him, stroking his shaft as he finally sucks my nipples into his mouth.

A miniature orgasm rushes through me, leaving me wired and desperate for more.

I whimper, "My pussy, you were going to lay me back over the couch—"

He takes my hand from his dick and then pushes me backward so that I fall. I land with my back on the cushions, my pelvis cock-eyed. Danny grabs my feet and tugs at me, until my pelvis is up and over the arm of the couch, just where he wants it. His blue eyes glitter with hunger as he stares down at me. He lowers his mouth and starts to kiss me down there. And I can watch him do it. I can see his eyes flick back up and gauge my responses. I can see his half-smile when he realizes he's done something I really like. I fist the couch and watch him eat me out.

My entire body grows hotter and I start to tremble. That's when Danny uses his fingers in tandem with his tongue, spreading me apart so he can lick directly on my clit. He hits the right spot and pulses his tongue.

The pressure turns into absolute mindless pleasure. My thighs clench around his face and my toes curl—I'm a sunbeam bursting through the clouds. Sensation overwhelms me and I shout, "Danny!" He keeps working, his tongue pulsing, eyes locked on me, until I start to fall limp.

I fall back on the couch in a daze and my eyes close. The next thing I know, Danny's pulling my hips back toward him. He's sheathed in a condom and he pushes inside me.

"This, yes, God! This," he breathes. And he strokes in and out of me hard. I watch him from the couch as he tosses my legs up over his shoulders and makes me his.

And after he's finished, he carries me into his room, full of kisses and promises for a round two. But he stops stock still when he flicks on the bedroom light and sees the chips all over his comforter.

"What the fuck happened in here?"

CHAPTER TWENTY-SIX

KATIE

Six Months Later

I unlock the apartment door and practically skip inside. I just signed up a new client. I get to organize a corporate party for Christmas. And I'm so, so excited. I almost start humming Christmas tunes. But humming out of season is one of Kenneth's pet peeves so I stop myself just as I enter the kitchen.

Kenneth doesn't look up from the powdered sugar he's sprinkling over a tray of tiny handmade pies. But he does smile. "I still heard you. 'I'm Dreaming of a White Christmas' is not allowed for seven more days."

"I stopped." I hold up my hands.

"Katie, it's okay to be annoying sometimes," he says as he finishes up. He blows me a kiss.

"Like you're being now?" At that jab, he does look back and I grin widely. "I couldn't help it. I got the job!"

"We got the job," he corrects me.

"You automatically assume I'm going to hire you to cater this new party? I don't know. This is New York. There are lots of five-star Michelin chefs here. Many of whom like Christmas carols any time of year."

Kenneth's grin spreads wider as he walks towards me. I love that grin. It still makes me go weak at the knees, even after we've lived together for months. He wraps his arms around my waist. He pulls me close and sways side to side with me in his arms. "You'd never hire anyone else."

"Maybe Heather's rubbing off on me."

"I'm gonna rub off on you." And he starts to. I feel him grow hard as he presses the hardness into my hip, up-and-down, up-and-down.

Hot anticipation builds in my stomach. "Oh are you? I thought we had agreed to wait for everyone tonight."

Kenneth leans down and tucks my hair behind my ear. He uses his tongue to trace the shell of my ear before he whispers, "I can't help if you're irresistible."

My hands fist in his shirt. "Alec's gonna be so mad if we don't wait. He should be on his way now ..." But even as I say those words, my hands are moving toward Kenneth belt.

Kenneth shrugs and just helps me undo his belt, pulling it open and popping the button on his pants. "So, you'll get in trouble. You know you like it when we spank you."

"Do you like getting spanked too?" I tease.

"We can find out," he responds.

I whimper as Kenneth's tongue moves onto my neck and traces over my sensitive pulse. His hands slide from my hips down to squeeze my hands.

"I have something for you," he says.

I reach the hard bulge in his pants and rub it as I say, "Give it to me."

As soon as I say those words, Kenneth's hands and mouth fall away. My eyes flicker open. He's already across the kitchen, bending over the tray of tiny, hand-made pies.

"When I said 'give it to me,' I didn't mean food," I roll my eyes. Even though about half of our sex sessions involve food, I was really ready for Kenneth to slide down and eat me instead of the pie.

"Do you remember that day on the island, when we were in Danny's villa?" he asks.

I straighten. Kenneth doesn't talk about the island much. The other guys do. But sometimes I think he'd rather forget all the dramatic shit that went down. So this is unusual. I walk toward him and say, "Yes?"

"You had caramel corn all over your skin. And Cheeto cheese. And fake candy fruit flavors." He gestures at the little pies. "I was feeling inspired when I thought about it. So ... new recipe. Happy six month anniversary, Katie."

Aw. The tears come to my eyes. But I try to hold them back, because if I start crying now, I'll be crying all night. My hand goes up to my heart and I say, "That's the sweetest. But I thought we said no gifts."

"It isn't a gift. It's just dessert."

I wag a finger at him as I snag one and bite into it. It's fucking amazing, just like everything Kenneth makes. Little apple pies with cinnamon and caramel inside and potato chip crumbles and cheese baked on top of the crust. "The guys are gonna be mad at you—" I warn.

"Mad at what?" Danny walks in and puts his helmet on the table with a thunk. He pops his neck. "Man, today was brutal. Ooh, snacks." He goes over to the counter and shoves a whole pie into his mouth.

"Do you need a massage, hun?" I ask him.

He shakes his head, his hair still wet from the shower at the station. "Nah, I'm good. We had ladder drills today. Practicing high-rise rescues."

"You should have told me, I would have come and watched." I imagine how his ass must have looked climbing up and down fire ladders all day. *Mmm.* The fact that Danny's training to be a New York City firefighter lights my fire. My eyes trace down his fitted t-shirt. Just seeing the logo on it gets me wet.

"You can stare at my ass anytime you want, babe. Plus, I knew you had that meeting. How'd it go?" he asks as he stuffs another pie in his mouth. He tosses Kenneth a thumbs up for the pie as he waits for my answer.

"We got it!" I do a happy shoulder shrug and Danny swoops me into his arms for a caramel apple-flavored kiss.

"You got what?" a deep voice says behind me.

I turn and wriggle out of Danny's arms so I can go hug Alec, who's still in his pilot uniform. He still flies private jets, but now he's based in the City so he can live with us. "I'm so happy you're home! How was your flight?"

He stares down at me. "Fuck that. It was a flight. Did you get the job?"

I nod. He swings me up into his arms and smacks my ass. "This calls for a celebration. How many orgasms should we give her, guys?"

"Six," Kenneth calls out.

"Nah, let's go for nine," Danny says. "Last time we did that, she nearly blacked out in bliss. Fucking awesome."

I wiggle and laugh, but I can't escape Alec's hold. "I thought we were going to anniversary dinner first!" I protest.

"Well, I mean ... we can move the reservation," Danny says as Alec carries me into the bedroom and tosses me on the bed. Danny and Kenneth are right behind us.

My men stare down at me, every one of them wearing shit-eating grins.

Heather's voice startles us all. "Hey y'all aren't having an orgy back there, are you?"

Kenneth narrows his eyes. "Giving her a key was a mistake."

"Well, considering she bought this apartment for us ..." I shrug.

Danny just sighs and his Oklahoman hospitality takes over. "We're in the bedroom, but we're still dressed!" he calls out. "Unfortunately."

Heather sashays in wearing her typical fall attire, a knee-length red trench coat and shiny black heels. She's gone all black with her hair, since she thinks that's big city style, but she can't let go of the big hair, so it falls down her back in epic curls. Andrew trails in behind her, wearing a suit. He stops in the doorway, but she heads right over, plops onto the bed, and gives me a hug. "So, did they give it to you yet!"

"Heather!" All three of my guys scold her immediately.

Her eyes go wide and her mouth opens into a perfect little 'O' of surprise. "Oops."

I turn and eye my guys curiously. Danny blushes; Kenneth's eyes glitter with mirth as he rebuckles his belt; and Alec's look is dark, intense, and penetrating.

I cross my arms. "I thought we agreed—no anniversary gifts."

"No, you said it was not fair if you had to get three anniversary gifts and they only had to get one," Heather corrects.

My face burns. "Heather! I told you that in confidence!"

She shrugs, not at all apologetic. "Well, it's true."

My guys just laugh.

"You're such a liar!" Danny grins. "You said you didn't care about gifts!"

"I don't! I feel spoiled already." Inside, I'm a bit pissed Heather outed me. Juggling a four person relationship is hard. And fucking hell! We've only done it for six months.

"Tell us the truth," Alec demands. "The reason you wanted the no gift rule."

I wring my hands and my eyes flicker down to the black bedspread. "What if I got you gifts and you hated them? Or worse—what if I got something one of you liked but someone else hated their gift? What if you thought I was playing favorites? What if you thought I was being more thoughtful to one of you—"

Kenneth looks smug. "Told you it was a favorites thing."

Danny and Alec groan. "Crap," they say, nearly simultaneously.

I furrow my brow.

Danny sighs. "We lost a bet. Now, we're both on dishes for a week."

Kenneth grins and rubs his hands together. "It's gonna be awesome. I've been holding back on you, Katie. Trying to minimize the prep work so you don't have as much to clean. But next week ..." he comes forward and kisses my hand, "I'm gonna make you the most exotic, complicated dishes I know."

I laugh. "Is that my gift? I'll take it. I think it's more fun for you than—"

"That's not your gift," Alec interjects. He unbuttons his pilot jacket and reaches for the interior pocket. He comes out holding a black, credit-card shaped square of metal. He passes it over to me. On the front, engraved into the metal, are the words "The Lab."

My eyebrows scrunch as I flip it over. There's no metallic stripe or little scratch-off silver code like on a gift card. I've never heard of this store, but then I've never heard of a quarter of the places in the City.

"Thank you?" It comes out as a question, and then I try to smooth over my asshole response with a smile. "I mean, you guys are sweet! I don't know this place, but I'm sure I'll have so much fun browsing—"

Danny waves a finger. "There will be *no* browsing!"

"What?" I search their eyes, even more confused.

Heather and Andrew are biting back full-on laughter.

"What is this place?" I ask, suspicion rising from my gut to swirl around my chest. "I'm not getting another tattoo!" I narrow my eyes at Alec.

He doesn't flinch. He just grins and pulls aside the neckline of his collar to proudly show off the "K" on his collarbone, a tat he got when he dared me to get the little palm tree that's on my hip.

I point a finger at him. "This better not be—"

Alec steps forward and grabs my hand. He kisses the tip of my finger, then sucks it into his mouth. He lets it pop back out before he says, "Katie, I don't repeat dares. I've told you that."

The way he words his statement makes my heart pound faster. Shit. Shit. So this is a dare. The fact that Kenneth comes around and hugs me from behind only ramps my anxiety up further. I feel like a wire in a set of braces that just got tightened. My eyes plead with Danny for relief, but he only looks excited to see me sandwiched between my other two boyfriends.

Kenneth gently pulls my hair behind me and holds it in a

ponytail with his hand. He bends to kiss one side of my neck. Alec kisses the other.

"Damn! That's hot!" Heather's voice interrupts the moment. I jump and slide away from both of them, holding the card out and pointing it accusingly at everyone.

"I could tit-slap you for ruining that," Danny grumbles at Heather.

"Only if you're man enough to follow it up," Heather taunts.

"Alright, calm down. Heather, I think we need to give them all a minute. I think we kinda jumped the gun, coming in before Katie was ready." Andrew grabs her by the elbow and leads her away.

To my surprise, she goes, though she whisper-protests the whole way out.

I turn back to my guys and cross my arms. "Well? What's this present that's not a present?"

"Stop pretending you aren't gonna like it, that's a lie," Danny says. "You've loved every damn dare you've ever done. It's gonna be awesome. And I'll be right there if you get nervous."

"If you're kissing ass hoping you'll be first, you've got another thing coming," Kenneth tells Danny.

"I should be first. I liked her first."

"I give her more foreplay," Kenneth responds.

"That's not—"

"Enough!" Alec silences their bickering. He comes toward me and takes the card from my hand. He holds it up in front of me. "Katie, this card will let you into the most exclusive sex club in the City."

My eyes widen in shock and fear, but other parts of me prickle with excitement. My breathing comes more shallow. "And …"

"And …" Alec draws it out by using the edge of the card to trace over my palm and up my arm. He gently runs it over my neck and up to my lips. He pulls the card away and waits until my eyes meet his.

I'm already panting. He already knows my answer. But I need to hear him say it.

"Katie, I dare you to go to this sex club with us."

My panties are drenched at those words. Every nerve ending is alive and buzzing and begging for Alec to touch me already. But he waits.

"Yes," I breathe.

Danny whoops, Kenneth claps, and Alec just smiles.

"DID SHE SAY YES?" Heather yells from the living room.

Danny rolls his eyes. "We're totally ditching her tonight."

That stops me short. "Wait. Heather's a member?"

Kenneth cocks his head. "Are you surprised?"

"Well, no. I guess. But I thought she picked Andrew."

Kenneth grins. "I've heard they like to get their freak on together onstage."

I roll my eyes. "Only Heather." My mind grinds to a halt and reverses, tires spinning as I realize the important part of that sentence. "There's a stage?"

Alec slips an arm around my shoulders and leads me out of the bedroom to the living room, where Heather and Andrew are waiting. "Don't worry. We aren't daring you to go on stage. Yet."

I put a hand to my eyes and shake my head. "Please don't ever—"

"She's coming!" Heather squeals, managing to jump up and down even though she's wearing four-inch stilettos.

"Not yet," Danny grins. Kenneth high fives him.

"Shut up, all of you," I roll my eyes as my guys grab their coats off the coat rack. Alec helps me shrug into mine. But I can't hold back a grin. My guys are looking giddy. Playful. Randy. That means a shit-ton of orgasms for me.

We head out into the hall and Heather presses the button for the elevator. "You're gonna love it, Katie. It's so bizzaro. There are people who dress up like Brazilian Carnival dancers with feathers and bring you drinks, a stage for drag queens, sex show theaters like plays, and—"

I put my hand to my mouth, a little overwhelmed. Intimidated would be an understatement. Kenneth pulls me into him and kisses my forehead. "Don't worry, Ruffles. We'll *ease* you into it."

I roll my eyes and say, "I just can't believe this is my life. My actual life."

"I know, right?" Heather says as the elevator dings and the

doors open. "Sometimes you get a happier ending than anything you ever could have planned."

Every single eye swivels to look at her with confusion.

"What? I'm deep." She glares at us and huffs as she stomps into the elevator and leans back against the little bar on the back. "Fine. My writer came up with it. But isn't it brilliant? And like, totally true."

I laugh. Heather's hired herself a ghostwriter to pen her autobiography. Which, of course she did, she's Heather.

Danny ushers me into the elevator, which is the first step on our next naughty adventure.

I laugh but say, "It is true though, H-bomb. I never thought I'd have a harem—"

My guys grin.

"And I never thought I'd only want one guy again, but ..." Heather puts a hand to her chest, and then exchanges a sweet smile with Andrew. "Sometimes fate's a clever bitch."

True that.

AFTERWORD

Thank you so much for reading! You are amazing, and you are the reason I can keep dreaming up beautiful worlds. If you liked this book, please leave an Amazon review and tell your friends!

Your reviews and recommendations keep me pumped up as I write the next books. So, thanks!

ACKNOWLEDGMENTS

A huge thanks to Rob, Raven, Ivy, Coralee, Kaydence, Rachel & Thais.

Another HUGE shout-out to all my readers out there. You guys keep me moving and writing! When I see you all chatting about the books in my Facebook group, it totally energizes and encourages me.

MORE BOOKS

My other reverse harem series is the Tangled Crown series. It's a medieval fantasy with a bully romance feel in the first book.

Tangled Crowns Series

Knightfall - Book 1 - Available Here

MidKnight - Book 2 - Available Here

If you liked the sense of humor in this story, you might want to check out my Paranormal Cozy mysteries. They are silly and snarky and full of laughs with a slow burn romance.

The Lyon Fox Mysteries

Magical Murder

Enchanted Execution

Supernatural Sleep

Hexed Hit

If you're in the mood for more intrigue, check out my Post-apocalyptic Thriller series.

Timebend

Melt

Burn

CONNECT AND GET SNEAK PEEKS

If you like to read exclusive snippets from different characters, make predictions with other readers, see my inspiration for books, or just come hang and be yourself, I have a Facebook reader group.

Feel free to join Ann Denton's Reader Group.

ABOUT ME

I have two of the world's cutest children, a crazy dog, and an amazing husband that I drive somewhat insane as I stop in the middle of the hallway, halfway through putting laundry away, picturing a scene.